Coming soon...

Jack Hunter
The French Connection

The second instalment in the riveting 'Jack Hunter' adventure series.

Dedication

Shaun 'Holly' Hollingsworth 1967 – 1986
A Great Friend

<u>Special Thanks</u>

Elliot Waite
Joshua Waite
Bethany Kendrew
Sam Lawton
Megan Gorton
Gail Lennon
John Butler

And

Zoe King

JACK HUNTER

Secret of the King

By

Martin King

First published in Great Britain 2011 by RAZOR SHARP.

A CIP catalogue record for this book is available from the British Library

Second Edition 2012

Printed and bound in the UK & US

ISBN 978 0 9571 0210 1

RAZOR SHARP Books.

Introduction

This book contains clues to a secret code-breaker. If you collect the letters at the beginning of each chapter, you will discover the location to where the code-breaker is hidden.

Find the clues

Unlock the secret

Solve the mystery

Discover the treasure

The Adventure Begins Now...

Chapter One

T

Jack sighed loudly; loudly enough for Mum and Dad to hear. He was twelve years old and no one ever asked his opinion, about anything. This move was the last straw.

The journey had been a nightmare. Two measly bananas and an out-of-date packet of Worcester sauce crisps, his least favourite flavour – was bad enough, but to be squashed tighter than a hamster in a matchbox for the longest journey in the world was the worst ever.

"Here we are, Jack, number fifty-six St Mary's Avenue, your new home." His mother's voice was bright with false cheerfulness.

Jack stared gloomily at the house. 'Great,' he muttered.

The outside walls were overlaid in vomit coloured pebbledash and the front door had been painted an ogre-green. The white plastic number six swung upside down by a single screw.

Jack climbed out of the car, just as the removal van pulled up.

The neighbours were already out in force pretending to work in their gardens or wash their cars.

His dad bore more of a resemblance to Mr.

Beanpole than Roger Hunter, as he unfolded his long wiry body out of the car, and smoothed down the single tuft of hair that grew out of the top of his head. He adjusted his thick-rimmed specs.

"Come on, Jacky," he shouted as he sprang to open the dilapidated gate. "Let's make hay while the sun shines."

Jack winced. He hated being called Jacky, because it made him sound like a girl. And he hated Dad's outdated expressions, 'make hay while the sun shines.' Yuk!

Jack looked around to see if anyone else had heard. Of course, they had! His dad had a voice like a foghorn.

Soon the removal men were unloading stuff from the lorry and carrying boxes and furniture into the house. Dad helped them while Mum directed operations.

Jack slunk around the house and into the back garden. He wasn't going to help move stuff. What was the point? He wasn't going to stay here. He was going to go back to Southend as soon as he could.

He wandered through the foot-high jungle of weeds and then limbo danced under a sagging clothesline. He heard a voice, just as he completed his move.

"Hello," a girl called out. Jack spun around and looked in every direction. "Over here," he heard her say.

A skinny girl with mousy-blonde hair and a pointed chin was leaning over the fence. She wore a mucky yellow, hand-knitted cardigan. It was so ghastly that Jack could only stare.

"So, you're the newbies?"

Jack frowned and didn't answer.

"I'm Jules," she said. Suddenly, she smiled and as she did so, her cheeks rounded like bubbles. "I'm eleven and I'm off to high school after the summer holidays. I'm gonna be in year seven." When Jack still didn't answer, she stuck her tongue out rolling up the edges.

She looked so funny that Jack laughed. He wasn't sure how to take this strange girl.

"Umm, that tongue thing it's pretty *sikk*."

"You talk funny," she said. "Are you from Wales? You are from Wales, aren't you, Welshy boy!"

Jack felt himself blushing. "I'm not from Wales; I'm from Southend."

"Southend? Never heard of it, but you must be brave though, moving into a haunted house."

"What are you on about?'

"Hasn't anyone told you? Mr. Gammon died in his sleep in that house three months ago. You don't want the front bedroom. Do you know which your bedroom is yet?"

"No," Jack replied his insides feeling like a bag of popcorn in the microwave that was about to explode.

"And Holly, that's my brother's best mate, swore

he saw the old man's ghost peering out the window only last week."

"I don't believe you."

"Yea, I swear it's true. My brother reckons he eats kids' brains."

"Oh yeah," he said, hoping he sounded unimpressed.

She nodded and then changed the subject, "How old are you?"

"Twelve."

"The same age as my brother, Martin. Will you be going to our school as well? You'll probably be in his class. Wait a minute and I'll go and find him."

"Er no need, I'm not staying," said Jack, wasting his breath. She was already tearing off and calling Martin's name.

"Jack…Jack where are you?" his dad shouted.

Jack loped back to the house.

"Where've you been? You need to tell the removal men where to put your stuff. Your bedroom is the one at the front of the house."

Chapter Two

H

Jack hardly slept that night and when he did, he dreamed about the weird girl and the ghost of Mr. Gammon. He felt tense and irritable when his mum shook him awake the next morning.

"Whart?" he moaned shoving the pillow back over his head. School holidays were all about sleeping in forever, not woken up at daft-o-clock.

"Come on Jack, get up."

"What for? It's the holidays."

"Because we're off to your grandad's," she explained. It rang a bell, but it was too early in the day to think and his head hurt from trying. Jack crawled out of bed. He did not want to go and see his grandad. He was the reason they had moved to this deadbeat place, so his mum could live near to her dad. Could he not have gone into a home with other old people?

As Jack stared out of the bedroom window, the girl from next door whizzed by on a red bike with a few kids in tow.

Mum was calling him, "Hurry up Jack, we'll be late."

He sighed, turned away and stomped down the stairs.

As he got into the car, he could hear the sound of

children's voices. Then the front seat groaned under the weight of his dad and the driver's door slammed shut as Mum got in behind the wheel.

"Why can't grandad look after himself?" Jack asked as they drove along the narrow lanes.

"Because he's old and frail and not too well," said Mum.

"Well how come he's so old?" Jack persisted.

"Because everyone gets old," his mother huffed.

"Will you and Dad get old as well?"

"Yes darling. Everyone does. Even you will."

"No chance, not me. I'm never going to get old," insisted Jack.

The overpowering smell of new air freshener caused Jack to feel sick. Just as he was about to ask for his mum to stop the car, she slowed down and turned into a street. The sign fixed on the side of a stone wall belonging to an old school read; Dam Head Road.

After a seventeen-point-parking manoeuvre, they walked through a powder blue gate into a small yard. There were a few pots in the yard, filled with colourful flowers and a small bench painted the same colour as the gate.

Jack followed his parents through the tiniest kitchen he had ever seen. It looked more like a corridor. Just then, he heard a cough—one of those deep, going-to-die-soon kind of coughs followed by a quivering voice. "Come in, come in."

Jack walked into the small, stiflingly hot living room. It looked as if time had stood still. It was so different from the house he lived in at Southend – or even the new house. The room cluttered with heavy, dark brown furniture had people from another age, wearing old-fashioned clothes, smiling out from framed photographs, all over the walls. The only modern piece was an impressive, fifty inch, flat screen television that overwhelmed the tiny room.

He noticed a picture of himself. It was last year's school photo and stood pride of place on a bureau pushed against the far wall.

Jack absorbed all this in seconds before hearing a sound, coming from a high-backed armchair in the darkest corner and he saw his grandad, sitting bolt upright in the chair. He had white hair and wrinkly skin but Jack noticed his eyes first. He had eyes that drilled into you and held your gaze.

His grandad looked overdressed for their visit wearing a shirt, tie, and royal blue blazer. Dozens of small badges covered the lapels of his jacket. Jack thought it was amazing that the old man could sit in a room with the fire on full and the sun cracking flags outside, and not break into a sweat. The heat was unbearable forcing Jack to take off his tracky top.

The adults chatted for a bit - Jack didn't listen, it was so boring - then his mum disappeared into the kitchen saying she was going to make sandwiches for lunch and his dad mumbled something about needing the loo and suddenly Jack was left alone with his grandad.

There was an awkward silence and then the old man leant forward.

"I'm glad you're here, boy," he said. "I need your help."

Jack frowned nervously. "What…?"

Grandad smiled. "But first," he said, "You must promise me not to tell your parents what I'm about to tell you."

"Yeah, OK, I promise," said Jack, humouring him.

'Daft old man, what's he on about?' he thought.

"Not a soul?"

Jack shook his head.

"This is a real story, Jack. A true story about…" he paused as if he was about to say something extremely important, "buried treasure!" (7)

Chapter Three

ES

Buried treasure! Two seconds ago, he had been praying for either his mum or dad to walk back into the room. Now, he hoped the cuckoo clock hanging on the wall would freeze time.

"Come closer young fella. I don't want to be having to shout—not at my age."

Jack obediently leaned closer to his grandad sat in the high-backed armchair. His grandad could be cool, almost.

"You have to understand, this is a secret I've never shared with anyone, ever. Not even my best friends knew about this. I've saved it for you," his grandad stated. Straightening himself amongst his cushions, he began his story.

"The year was 1951 and I'd just finished school. I wasn't much older than you are. We left school a lot younger back in them days. We were in the middle of a heat wave and on this particular day, I was out playing in Knowles field with my two best mates Billy and Frank.

We always managed to find something to do. Not like you young ones today. You have computers, the internet, mobile phones, but you still loiter in the streets with nothing to do. Apparently it's because you're bored," his grandad began to drift.

Jack tried to conceal a yawn. "Don't worry, son," his grandad noted, "I'm getting to the good bit now.

We discovered bulldozers and diggers in one of the farmer's fields. At the time, we didn't know it, but the field was being levelled to make way for a golf course. The machinery wasn't in use at the time and there were no workers around.

By teatime, the skies were black as thunder, a storm was brewing you see and it was coming in fast. Billy and Frank wimped off home before the rain started. Pair a girl's blouses or what, eh? Well I stayed behind. It wasn't every day you got to climb up on top of a dirty, great big bulldozer and drive it."

"Wow, you actually got to drive it? Had they left the keys in the ignition?" Jack interrupted.

"No, no," grandad chuckled. "I was just pretending to drive it.

So there I was, sitting on top of the bulldozer when I felt a few drops of rain. The heavens opened up right above my head. I jumped off and pegged it down the field towards the old oak tree halfway down the hill when it happened..."

"Jack, how many sandwiches do you want?" his mum called from the kitchen.

"None," he shouted.

"Are you sure?" she asked again.

"Yes!" Jack huffed.

"So what happened next, Grandad?"

"Steady on, I'm getting to that now. The rain was

pounding in my face. My eyes were stinging and I couldn't see properly. I'd nearly made it to shelter when I slipped. At first, I thought I had just slipped in the mud, or worse still, a cowpat. The whole ground underneath me was trembling, shaking like a mini-earthquake. I wondered what the dickens was happening. The ground opened up beneath me and I fell.

I laid there for a moment, more shocked than hurt. When I jumped up, I figured I was in a whole heap of trouble. Worse still, I was dripping wet and covered in mud and I knew my mum would kill me when I got home," his grandad explained.

"I tell you, a right royal battleaxe and fiery temper to match she was, but a heart of solid gold." Jack willed his grandad to get back to the treasure.

"It was then that I noticed the tunnel," grandad continued. "I wished for the world, I had a torch with me. It was impossible to see anything."

"What kind of tunnel, like a secret passage or something? Did it take you into another world?"

"No, no. The tunnel was old, very old. The lightning strikes lit inside the tunnel; it appeared to travel as far as the eye could see. It was big enough for me to stand up in. I tried to leap up and touch the ceiling, but it was too high. There were paintings hanging along the walls and even suits of armour."

"What, you mean like knights in shining armour?" Jack interrupted again.

"Yes, just like knights in shining armour. You could tell the whole thing was very old, ancient in fact. It had that funny smell about it, sort of sulphur. You know the smell – that whiff you get when you bash two bits of limestone rock together."

Jack nodded in acknowledgement. He remembered the teacher mentioning something once in his chemistry class.

"The section that caved in must have been caused by the weight of the heavy bulldozers. I was just about to climb out, when I saw it. At first, I thought my eyes were playing tricks on me in the shadows. But, then, I was sure I saw what looked like a box—a small casket. After some effort, I managed to scramble over to it. And there it was..."

"What was there, Grandad?" Jack was desperate to know.

"A wooden box...a treasure box! Excited, I tried to pick it up, but it was too heavy. I pulled one of the small bricks from the pile of rubble and used it to smash the box open..."

"Are you telling him more of your sea-faring stories dad?" asked Jack's mum as she appeared with a tray of sandwiches and a small plate of Cadbury's mini rolls. "If you want a mini roll Jack, you'll have to have at least one sandwich first," she said putting the tray on a fold out table next to Jack, placing the chocolate rolls right under his nose.

"I didn't know you were in the war Grandad?"

"No Jack," grandad half laughed and half coughed, "I was too young. I was born at the beginning of the Second World War and lived through it as a kid. Those were crazy days, but that's for another time. No, I went into the merchant navy when I was old enough. If you wanted to travel the world and get paid for the privilege, that's what you did back then."

Earlier that day Jack would have done anything to get out of visiting his grandad, but only a few hours later, all he wanted to do was sit and talk about the treasure. In fact, where was the treasure? Did he have it stashed in the house somewhere? Even better, did he want to give it to Jack?

The afternoon soon passed and it was time to leave. "Oh Jack," his grandad called after him. "I've got a little something for you."

Jack's heart skipped a beat in delight. Real gold! Diamonds! Without having to get up from his chair, grandad leaned towards the perfectly positioned bookshelf. Besides stacks of books, the shelves were full of ornaments and junk. "Here you go your very own key-ring torch. You never know when it might come in handy, if you know what I mean."

How disappointing. The short, dumpy-looking object was not what he expected. He rolled it around in his fingers but could not find an on/off switch anywhere.

"You twist it," his grandad explained. As Jack did,

a bright, pale blue light shone directly in his eyes, nearly blinding him.

'Message to brain: Next time you turn on a torch, make sure it's pointing in the opposite direction.'

"Oh, and Jack, make sure you come back and visit. We have unfinished business." Jack was sure he saw his grandad wink. The man he had met earlier that day had been a complete stranger, but the one now sitting in that armchair was, his grandad. (19)

Chapter Four

E

The next day was rubbish with a capital R. Jack climbed off his bed, fought his way pass piles of unpacked boxes and drew back the drab green and brown stripe curtains. Water streamed down the glass as the rain hammered against the window.

A visit to his Grandad Green was not on the agenda today. Jack was desperate to find out about the treasure. The thought of it stashed in his grandad's attic or hidden in his bedroom was fantastic.

Bored, he turned to face the mountain of boxes. He was supposed to be unpacking but could not be bothered. He had just spent the last couple of hours playing FIFA, but even that had limits.

Thomas Edison step aside, Jack just had a brainstorm. It is impossible to keep a master schemer down. If he crammed all his belongings into his drawers, wardrobe and even under the bed, he would be finished in minutes, if not seconds. Then he would be free to watch TV.

The only flaw in this otherwise-brilliant plan was ten minutes became two hours.

Finally, he had finished. With a victorious spring in his step, he managed the bottom six steps in one enormous leap; and narrowly avoided a bone-crunching collision with the front door.

There was nothing on TV. Jack wondered if there was a national conspiracy among the networks, to air all the junk programmes when it was bad weather. They knew you had to watch it anyway. They saved all the best programmes for Friday and Saturday nights, forcing you to stay in, even if you had other plans.

Bored, Jack decided to settle for a game of indoor football, a tennis ball or golf ball would suffice. If only he knew which box to look in.

A wooden shelf affixed to the wall displayed his mum's entire collection of three glass ornaments. Jacks eyes rested on one of the crystals – the one that looked more like a replica golf ball than a cut-glass crystal.

'I am your best friend; you can use me,' the precious ornament called out to him.

Jack wasn't naughty, just easily led. He had to think this through; his mum had just nipped to the shop. If he took two cushions from the sofa and positioned them carefully against the wall at the end of the living room below the window, his mum's crystal would be safe.

Seconds later, he was in the World Cup dribbling past three defenders. "Hunter gets the ball, goes past one and then another...looks up, and shoots..." Jack could only watch as the prized football managed to find its way past the two cushion goalies through the only gap possible.

CRASH! His mum's pride and joy hit the wall and shattered into half a dozen pieces. His life flashed before him as his fate was sealed.

A flash of inspiration led Jack to his dad's toolbox. Super glue!

Being extra careful not to get any glue on his fingers – he remembered his friend Jimmy Farnaby getting half a model plane stuck to his head and had to be taken to hospital to have it removed – the round cut-glass ornament sat proudly in its position on the shelf as good as new, well almost.

That night, his mum came to say goodnight. He prayed she hadn't spotted anything unusual about her prize crystal. Jack held his breath as she began to speak.

"Tomorrow, luvvie, if you don't mind," she said, "I thought we could go to your grandads again. I have to do some cleaning."

Excitement has a strange affect on children and Jack was unable to sleep...for hours.

***

The following morning dragged. Finally his mother said that magic word, 'grandad.' He was already fully dressed and standing by the door with his trainers on before his mum could blink. Normally, his parents would be waiting for him.

They complained he only had one gear. Slow!

The wait was finally over and they were pulling into an empty parking space a few doors down from his grandad's house.

This time around, Jack was not as nervous. He was happy to see his grandad again. Yet there was one major problem. His mother had inadvertently forgotten to mention one important piece of information to Jack – his grandad was out.

"What do you mean he's gone for a check-up?" Jack berated his mother.

"Well he goes every Tuesday to the doctors. That's why we've come to do the cleaning. While he's out we can get more done."

"What!!! You mean I've got to help as well?" Jack wailed in dismay.

"I did tell you..." his mother began.

"I know," Jack interrupted her. "But I didn't know you meant I had to clean as well. I was looking forward to seeing grandad."

Jack knew he was fighting a losing battle. His mum seemed to ignore every word he said.

Assigned to vacuum duty, he entered his grandad's bedroom – his inner sanctum. A chest of drawers stood either side of the bed with a large, antique wardrobe set back against the opposite wall. A shabby looking teddy bear sat all alone in the middle of a rocking chair.

As Jack fired the vacuum into life, he tried to

picture what it must be like to be a billionaire; with so much money, it was impossible to spend it. Why, if his grandad had a vast fortune in gold and diamonds, did he choose to live in this crummy place?

Just then, an interesting thought occurred to Jack. His grandad might have hidden the treasure in the house. In this, very room. He began to look round for a likely place. There was nothing under the bed. If Jack wanted to hide something valuable, where would he hide it?

Of course, on top of the wardrobe!

The top of the wardrobe had an ornate plinth making it difficult to see if anything was up there. Jack stood on his tiptoes, he was certain he caught a glimpse of something. He scoured the room for anything strong enough to support his weight.

His gaze rested on the rocking chair once more. It would be difficult trying to balance on it. But, if the treasure was up there...

Jack pulled the big, old rocker across in front of the wardrobe and attempted to stand on it. It almost felt like being at sea, as he wobbled from side to side.

Nestled on top of the wardrobe was a large tan leather suitcase. Thick layers of dust covered it and the edges were starting to crack. He grabbed the case and tried lifting it. It was so heavy he was sure it contained something valuable.

As he gave the suitcase an almighty heave, he

tumbled backwards. Fortunately, the bed broke his fall. He paused for a second in case his mother had heard the noise. Wheezing from the exertion, he laid the case safely on the bed. Luck was with him. The suitcase did not have either a padlock or a security combination to secure it. His heart was pounding; he took a couple of deep breaths before he opened it.

"Jack," his mum called, "what are you doing?"

"Nothing..." quickly he fumbled the fasteners shut. All that stress for a suitcase packed with old clothes. How could he have been so daft? Even to think that there would be treasure hidden in his grandad's bedroom.

Pushing the rocking chair into place, he spotted a small wooden door, a secret door. It was about the size of a kitchen cupboard and normally hidden from view by the chair. Covered in wallpaper, the camouflaged door looked almost invisible.

Behind the door was a cupboard. Inside was a very old box. It looked exactly how he imagined a pirate's treasure chest would be. Metal straps bound the wooden panels in place. A tarnished brass lock with an engraving of a cross inside a circle concealed its contents from prying eyes. He had found it!

Before he could decide on his next move, he heard his mum call again, only this time she sounded nearer. "What on earth are you doing?" she snapped as he pushed the rocking chair into place.

"Erm... I'm just... er putting the chair back after,

erm... vacuuming behind it," he replied, sounding guilty even to his own ears.

"Well done!" she congratulated him. "But you can leave it for now and come downstairs, your grandad's home." Result!

Half an hour later nothing was going to plan. Jack ached inside but his mother would not leave the two of them in private. When finally she left the room to finish cleaning upstairs Jack hoped this would be it, but his grandad avoided the important subject of the treasure. Instead, he rambled on about being in the navy and his other children – Jack's aunty and uncles – and he even mentioned his allotment.

What was so interesting about growing vegetables on a plot of land somewhere else? Jack wanted to hear more about the treasure and the secret chest.

"Now where were we?" his grandad asked. Jack suddenly sat upright like an obedient dog waiting for a treat from its master. "Oh yes, I was telling you all about the secret gold. So Billy and Frank decided to run home because of the storm..."

"You've already told me that grandad... You were in the tunnel," Jack prompted.

"Have I? Oh, yes, so I have. Where was I then? The box, I spied a box." Jack had heard that bit too, but did not want to interrupt again.

"I fumbled around in the dark for a brick and smashed the lock; the latch broke in my hand. I hesitated for a second, my thoughts on all kinds of riches locked away in that wooden chest. I could be rich. Then I couldn't contain myself any longer. With a mind of its own, my hand thrust back the lid and opened the box.

I couldn't believe my eyes. A small fortune in gold coins and jewels the size of golf balls, pearl necklaces and other precious gems. Then a flash of lightening temporarily lit up the tunnel and everything sparkled, glistened as if it was all brand new."

His grandad paused to catch his breath. "I pulled out an ornate globe bigger than a cricket ball and by the weight of it, made from pure solid gold. I remembered it adorned with countless gems and a golden cross on the top. It was almost identical to the piece they call 'the Sovereigns Orb' from the crown jewels."

"So, have you got it grandad? Can I see it? Can I, please?" Jack pleaded, his excitement bubbling over.

Even if his grandad had not been able to carry most of it back, that golden globe thing alone must be worth millions!

"Oh, no son, I haven't got it," his grandad said as cool as you like.

"Well where is it?" Jack asked, knowing there must be a logical explanation.

"I left it there."

"Did you bring the gold coins instead, then?"

"No. I left them there too," his grandad explained, as though it was the most sensible thing to have done.

"It was raining and dark you see and besides, it was too heavy for me to carry. I planned to come back with a coal sack and my handcart. However, when I returned home, I was grounded for a week. By the time I managed to sneak back after school, the hole had disappeared. They had bulldozed the whole field and turned it into a golf course. Even the oak tree was gone."

"So you didn't get the treasure?" Jack was gobsmacked.

'And if not, what about the chest upstairs,' Jack thought.

"No. Well, I looked. Time after time, I went back, digging little holes on the golf course. The secret was to make it look like moles you see, so no one would suspect what I was doing."

Jack heaved a sigh of disappointment.

"...but anyway, when I say I didn't take any of the treasure, I guess that wasn't entirely true." Jack looked up. He watched intently as his grandad reached for a book off his bookshelf.

His grandad slowly pulled something from inside the pages. It was small and round, the size of a coin. His wrinkled fingers trembled. The light flooded from the window, causing the object to glint.

If Jack was not mistaken, this was no ordinary coin. It was pure gold. (22)

Chapter Five

C

"I did pick up one coin," his grandad continued.

Jack's gaze followed the coin's hypnotic movement. Finally, his grandad's outstretched hand hovered tantalisingly in front of Jack's face, sending him cross-eyed. "Here, take it then..."

The gold coin looked brand new—surprising for its age—and about the size of a ten pence piece. Holding it between trembling forefinger and thumb, Jack examined the glistening coin. On the back were three lions but no words, no inscriptions or any other markings that might reveal some clue.

Flipping the coin around instead of seeing a traditional monarch's head wearing a crown was a picture of a cross. The body of the cross was circular with a diamond shape cut in its centre. A half moon and a star were engraved either side of the diamond.

"So what do you reckon then? Do you like it?" his grandad asked breaking the silence.

"Um...yeah," Jack stammered. "I mean, of course I do, grandad. It's well good."

"Well, it's yours."

"What? You mean I can have it?" Jack nearly dropped the coin.

"I've been hanging on to it all this time, waiting to give it to you. For years, I tried to find that treasure again. It became an obsession. Everywhere I turned, I just kept drawing blanks. Then Muriel came into my life, your grandmother, bless her. Soon after, we were married followed by children and that I'm afraid, put paid to that. Mind you, I did try sneaking up there a couple of times.

Then your mother gave birth to you and, from the moment I first saw you, I could see in your eyes you were a Green. I knew then that I would tell you my secret one day. You need to keep it somewhere safe; you never know when light-fingered Harry might be around."

At first, Jack was lost for words. Being told a story about untold riches and shown the gold coin—proof it was all real—well, that was brilliant. And then, to discover this was now his special secret, his duty to carry on the search – one-hundred-percent epic!

"But I...er, great. Thanks," was all he could muster.

"You'll do it won't you? I need you to take over where I left off."

"Of course I will grandad."

"But remember, not a word to your parents – or to anyone else."

***

Once home, Jack rushed straight to his room. Making sure he closed the door securely behind him, he jumped onto his bed with such a leap, the bounce nearly threw him off the other side. This room was bigger than his room in the old house, which was a result apart from the walls that were covered in cow-poo coloured wallpaper.

He unzipped his tracksuit pocket, pulling out the piece of tissue he had wrapped around the coin. He laid the coin in his palm and watched it gleam as the sun streamed in through the bedroom window.

Jack knew he had seen the picture before. He searched through the inner storage compartments of his brain.

That was it!

Jack rummaged around in the top drawer. 'Ah, here it is' he thought, pulling out his football world cup sticker book. Impatiently, he turned the pages. 'France...no, gone too far. Here we go, England.'

His eyes rested on the team emblem: the three lions. That was it. Why would this coin have the same motif as a football logo? Was it some FA cup winner's medallion?

Jack stared blankly at the coin, baffled by it all. Not only that, here he was, on the verge of the greatest discovery he could imagine, and yet he was unable to share his secret. If only his best mate, Matthew Thompson was here, he would have someone with whom to share his new secret. (8)

Chapter Six

RE

Jack travelled the seven seas hunting pirates' treasure before finally arriving home by steering the ship up his street to bury his haul under the sofa. To his dismay, he awoke to find he was still in his bedroom.

Sat in the living room eating his breakfast Jack found it impossible to get his grandad's story out of his head. It ran round and round in his mind like a hamster in its wheel. A knock at the door broke his thoughts.

"Hi, is Jack in?" a girl's voice asked. Leaving his last spoonful of cereal, he moved through the house swifter than an owl swooping on a poor, unsuspecting dormouse. He moved so fast his mum barely had chance to call his name.

"Yeah," he panted. "I can, can't I, mum?" he said before dashing upstairs to get his trainers.

"Your mum's pretty cool," said Jules, hopping like a frog over the breaks in the flags on the path. Jack watched as she bent her knees and sprang onto the next one. He did not intend to copy her. He wondered why she was carrying a lettuce but decided that it was best not to ask. They wandered next door to Jules' house.

The back garden at number fifty-eight looked like a small field — perfect for footie — with a set of swings at the bottom and a wooden hut with a window made out of chicken wire in one corner. There was not a single flower – not of the cultivated kind anyway – apart from a few, random dandelions dotting the lawn, but weeds did not count.

It turned out Lola the one-eyed rabbit lived in the hutch – that is according to Martin. Jules defended her rabbit by pointing out Lola actually had two eyes, but was partially blind. A mental picture of a pirate rabbit with a patch over one eye flashed through Jack's head as he watched Jules put the lettuce in the hutch – so that's what it was for.

"So you're Jack, then," the boy said. "I'm Martin, Jules' older brother." Jack had guessed as much. The older boy was the spitting image of Jules, only taller with freckles. Before Jack could respond, Martin ran off.

"Where's your brother gone?" he asked Jules.

"Probably to see if Holly the boy-dustbin is around," Jules laughed.

"What? A boy called Holly?" Jack asked.

"It's short for Hollingsworth. But, whatever you do, don't wind him up about having a girl's name. He turns into the Hulk," warned Jules. Jack saw what she meant as the two boys appeared. Holly was bigger than Jack in every direction.

"Look everyone," Martin announced, grabbing Holly's wrist and lifting it into the air. "Holly's got a girly bracelet."

"It's not," he protested, wrenching his arm free. "It's a present from my uncle and it's an historic Incan amulet from Peru if you don't mind."

Jack sat on one of the swings rocking, trying hard not to laugh. Holly seemed a proper geekoid, nothing like how Jules had described him.

Martin skipping and jumping rushed towards the conifer trees at the bottom of the garden. Jack rubbed his eyes as Martin disappeared. Holly followed and before Jack could say anything, Holly vanished too.

He turned to Jules for answers who simply replied, "Shortcut."

Jack followed Jules to the same spot where he had watched the two boys disappear. There was nothing there except thick, green foliage. He closed his eyes and stepped forward. The prickly needles brushed against his hands and face. Once through, he opened his eyes to see a ten-foot-high fence right in front of his nose. If he had taken another step, he would have slammed straight into it.

Jack squeezed between the hedge and the fence until he turned a corner to find an open gate. He found himself in the biggest garden he had ever seen. Lawns stretched as far as he could see. A tall weeping willow partially hid the large house at the opposite end of the lawn. He spotted the others jogging towards a summerhouse, shaped like a fifty-pence piece.

Seconds later, he caught up with them just as Holly opened the double doors. "Ta-da! What do you think, impressive or what?" Holly asked. Inside the summerhouse besides the black leather sofas and a fridge stacked with cans of pop, was a cool looking plasma TV that took up one wall.

"Wow! What does your uncle do?" Jack gawped.

"I don't know really, something to do with rare antiques. He's away quite a lot. But, we've even got Wi-Fi," Holly bragged.

"That's brilliant!" Jack enthused. "Can I have a go on your laptop when you've finished? I need to find out about the treasure."

"What treasure?" all three of them asked at once. Whoops! Jack had let his closely guarded secret slip.

Grandad Green had specifically said not to tell anyone. Jack wanted to make his grandad proud and not let him down; on the other hand, they had allowed him entry into their exclusive gang. Now he was one of them he told them what his grandad had said, and then pulled out the gold coin.

"Wouldn't it be so cool if we could find the treasure?" cheered Martin.

"Don't be daft, it could be anywhere," Jules said crushing Martin's enthusiasm.

"Hang on. There's an inscription on the side of this coin!" Holly exclaimed.

"Let me have a look?" Martin demanded, leaping towards Holly.

"It looks something like A-D-M-E-R-G-I-L-L," Holly spelled.

"And what's that mean when it's at home?" asked Jack.

"If anyone will know, then Mr. History Geek in the corner will," Martin laughed pointing at Holly. "But I'm sure I recognise that name from somewhere."

"Don't be daft, Martin," Jules mocked him. "You're useless at history and geography."

"No, honest! I have," he protested.

"Whatever," she dismissed him waving her hand in the air.

Holly's face looked like a bulldog as he concentrated. Jack grabbed a drink out of the fridge to take his mind away from the agony of waiting. It felt like fireworks were exploding inside him. They were about to find out where the treasure was buried and, he had found friends to help him.

"Right. Let's take a look at what we've got," said Holly. He began tapping away at the keyboard.

Jack, Jules, and Martin inched closer around the desk where Holly sat.

"Admergill is a family name from around Blacko and Barrowford by the looks of it. Mainly from the sixteenth and seventeenth centuries," Holly informed them, peering at the screen.

"Where's Blacko and Barrow-whatsee-said?" Jack asked.

"They're two villages about six or seven miles away," Jules explained.

"I've been to Barrowfor..."

"Wait a minute," Holly interrupted Martin. "This looks interesting..."

"What?" they all shouted at once.

"Now then, you scoundrels, what are you up to?" a voice boomed.

Jack spun round to see a man about the same age as his dad, but smartly dressed – and with hair.

"Uncle." Jack watched as Holly jumped up to receive a big hug.

"So which country have you been to this time?" Holly asked.

"I haven't," Holly's uncle roared with laughter, after dropping Holly back on his feet. "I've been to Cornwall. I've brought you all some Cornish fudge. Do you want to come back up to the house for it?"

"Great, Mr. King," Martin leapt forward.

"Ha-ha! How many times do I have to tell you? Just call me Simon."

"Well anyway Uncle Simon, we haven't time," said Holly. "We're busy on a treasure hunt."

Jack almost fell over. When Holly's uncle left, he rushed straight over to him. "What you doing telling him about our secret?"

"What? Relax mate," soothed Holly. "We do stuff like this all the time. He thinks we're just messing about."

"Even so, next time, don't! Alright..." Jack fumed.

"When you two have finished arguing, I've found a website that mentions about Admergill in Barnoldswick," Jules cut in. "It's on the official Lancashire historical website."

"Let's look then..." Jack rushed over to hear more. Martin was busy jumping up and down on a beanbag.

"It mentions he had a vaccary in Barnoldswick way back in 1395."

"What's a vaccary when it's at home?" Jack wanted to know.

"I thought you were from near London? Aren't you supposed to be all educated down there? A vaccary is a sort of shed where they keep cows," Jules said.

"Yeah," Jack defended not knowing whether Jules was serious or not, "but they don't have cows and that in London, do they? And besides I'm from Southend – which is next to the sea, actually." (22)

Chapter Seven

T

It seemed impossible that four children could create so much noise. After the buzz died down, Jack felt a slight hiss of air leaking from his treasure bubble. He was desperate for his grandad's story to be true, but all the information they found offered no help.

A paper missile narrowly missed Jack's head. He spun round to see a guilty-looking Martin. Soon the others were becoming bored too and wanted to be out in the sun. It was more like a dictatorship than a democracy. Jack had no alternative but to go with them.

They were on the verge of the most amazing thing to happen to them – if not to any school kid, ever – and yet Martin wanted to mess around outside.

Soon, the four of them wandered to the end of their street and came to a narrow, country lane. A field dipped into a hollow before sprawling over the horizon. Jack thought this was cool, back home it was just concrete for miles. They did have the sea nearby, but it was cold and dirty.

Holly nearly stepped on a frog. Jules quickly shoved everyone out of the way, picked up the frog and popped the tiny amphibian into her pocket. Martin explained to Jack that she often brought home small animals, building houses for them in their back garden and even in her bedroom.

They turned left down the lane. Straight away, Jack could see the farm. The farmyard was just what he expected. A rusty, red metal gate barred the entrance. Quick as a flash, the other three climbed up the bars and sat on top. Then the real excitement kicked in. They sat there!

Holly pulled something from his pocket that crackled noisily. Seconds later, he was crunching on a packet of crisps. 'Of all the flavours to be eating at a farmyard,' thought Jack, 'smoky bacon.' Although Holly was bigger than Jack and Martin, amazingly, he was a whole month younger.

Jack had never been to a farm before and he now realised why. The whole place had the same unpleasant stench as a sewage factory. The others seemed oblivious to the smell. Jack watched in bemusement as Jules kept talking to the frog in her pocket.

"Oh, no, look whose coming?" Martin squealed.

Jack glanced up the lane to see a beefy lad wearing a scruffy green coat, ripped jeans and a pair of Doc Marten boots heading towards them. A gangly-legged, skinny dog trotted alongside his heels.

"It's the Stoneman!" Martin huffed.

By this time, the boy who looked at least in year ten was upon them. "So who's this moron hanging out with you, Browny?" he demanded. "In fact, don't tell me, I can't be bothered today. I'm off rabbiting."

He gave the metal gate a forceful shove before walking away laughing to himself. Jack toppled backwards. A vision of farmyard poo covering his favourite top flashed before his eyes. Luckily, Holly had surprisingly quick reflexes. In a flash, he grabbed Jack's arm and stopped him from falling.

"Who was that idiot?" Jack grumbled. He was starting to feel nauseous.

"The Stoneman," Holly explained, pulling a strawberry lace out of his pocket. "He's your typical, class 'A' bully."

"His nickname probably has a lot to do with his prehistoric approach to life," Jules pointed out.

"And you won't believe how old he is? He's in our year at school!" Martin explained.

Jack groaned, knowing his luck he would end up in the same class.

"You will love it in history," enthused Holly. "Mr. Booth is brilliant..."

"Are you mad or what?" Martin interrupted. "History is for wimps."

"If it wasn't for history, then we wouldn't know anything about Admergill being from Lancashire would we? That's real history, anyway I've been thinking about it..."

"You don't say," interrupted Martin.

"Do you realise that when you grow up without an education, you will end up without a job and no money," Holly pointed out.

"And did you know *dammit I'm mad* backwards is, *dammit I'm mad*?" Martin responded looking around to see if the others appreciated his witty remark.

"As I was saying," Holly continued pretending not to have heard. "Don't you think it's strange that King Richard was mates with a commoner from the North?"

"And what's wrong with that?" Jack asked.

"Well, back then kings didn't mix with the lower classes. I can't put my finger on it, but something..."

"The barn," Martin blasted out, nearly falling off the gate. "I told you I'd seen that name before."

"What are you on about? You don't know anything about history," dismissed Jules.

"Well, you don't need to be brainy to know stuff. You know the old barn, well that's got that Adamerry-gill word carved into the stone over the door."

"Martin, you're a genius," Jack crowed.

"I wouldn't go that far," mocked Jules. Holly turned away unimpressed by Martin's observational luck rather than showing intelligence.

Jack jumped off the gate. "So what are we waiting for?"

Chapter Eight

O

Jack and his friends ran towards the barn. They turned onto a bumpy, pothole-infested, side road, covered with stone chippings.

"Jack? Knock, Knock..." Martin asked.

"Who's there?"

"Anna."

"Anna who?"

"Anna-body know any good jokes? Ha-ha." Martin turned to run away, and tripped in a pothole. His face instantly turned bright crimson.

Trying not to laugh at Martin's pathetic joke, Jack noticed a grey stone barn. It was the oldest building he had ever seen. It looked as though it could topple over with the slightest gust of wind. The roof made from large stone flags covered in moss, sagged in the middle. Even he could have done a better job.

Jack and Jules caught up with Martin. Sure enough, above the large, wooden doors was a flat, smooth stone with the word ADMERGILL. Just below was a stone shield with the three lions emblem carved into it. Underneath were the letters MCCCXCV.

"What year do the Roman numerals say?"

"Thirteen-ninety-five, I think," replied Jules.

"Wow! I can't believe this is over five hundred

years old," exclaimed Martin.

"Six," Jules pointed out.

"You what?" asked Martin confused.

"Six. It's over six hundred years old." Jules pointed out.

"I know that," Martin defended. "But I was right. Six-hundred is over five-hundred years and that is what I said."

Jules threw her hands in the air, while Martin stood grinning triumphantly just as Holly caught them up, more interested in finishing his double chocolate-chip muffin than running at full pelt.

"Do you know what, I've never noticed that before and to think I could have used this in my last history project," Holly announced, unaware the others were completely disinterested.

Treasure hunting was worse than being on a rollercoaster, one minute a new revelation followed by hours of boredom. He was itching to get inside the barn and find the gold. The only thing between Jack and his destiny were the large, wooden doors, fastened by a chain and held together with an enormous padlock.

Martin went around the side of the building, Jack followed. Ten foot up was a window with no glass, cut into the side. Looking as though they had done this a thousand times before, Martin and Holly dragged an old, rusty gate lying on the ground and leaned it against the side of the barn. They had turned the gate into a ladder; now they had a way in.

"You need to be careful 'cause you never know when the farmer will turn up," Martin explained.

Jack was not keen on the idea. He watched as Jules scampered up the metal gate and through the hole before he could blink.

"He's chained the doors up, but he doesn't realise we still can get in," Martin said. "You next then," he gestured to Jack.

There was no backing out—especially after Jules had just done it. She was a whole year younger. Jack's legs shook as he inched up the rusting frame. Relieved, he reached the small opening and crawled through.

Jack saw the remains of a tractor, half parked, half collapsed in a heap just underneath him. It looked difficult, but Jules was watching. Bracing himself, he jumped onto the tractor's roof, then onto its bonnet before finally swinging down from its tire-less front wheel. He was surprised how easy it was.

Jack had just landed on the ground and dusted himself off when he heard a thud behind him. He spun around to see Martin grinning like a Cheshire cat. "What was that?" Jack wanted to know as Holly suddenly poked his head through the gap in the wall.

"We can't let the farmer know we're in here," Martin explained. Holly had pushed their temporary ladder onto the ground.

"But how are we supposed to get out?" Jack

asked.

"Just jump. It's not far," Martin replied nonchalantly. To avoid looking like a chicken, Jack decided not to protest.

The inside of the barn was no prettier than the outside. There was the pile of junk that resembled a tractor, a few bales of hay, and a rusted feeding trough with a large hole in its belly. Jules swung back and forth on a thick piece of rope that someone had tied to a long, wooden beam.

After searching in vain for clues, the others became more interested in playing. Before long, they were swinging on the rope and messing around in the broken-down tractor. They had their very own private playground.

The bright sunshine outside highlighted the gaps in the flagged roof. As laser beams of light shone into the barn, Jack noticed small pieces of chaff dancing in and out through the shafts of light. Morning became lunchtime, which in turn, became mid-afternoon until finally it was nearly teatime. Suddenly, Jack realised how hungry he was.

"I dare you to climb up the rope, Jack," Jules challenged.

She had just placed Jack in an awkward predicament. He was not a wimp, but had to think fast. "Only if you do it first," he replied, quite pleased with his quick riposte.

Before Jack could gloat any further, Jules shot up

the rope like a spider monkey, touched the beam and shimmied back down all in one flowing movement. What could he do now? Martin shoved him in the back and gave a few hearty words of encouragement.

Jack stretched his hands up, grabbed hold of the thick rope and gave it an unconvincing tug. He held his breath and heaved himself upwards. His heart pounded hard against his ribcage while sweat poured from his forehead. He was afraid to release a hand to wipe away the perspiration for fear of slipping.

Jack reached the top of the rope. The ordeal had exhausted him. He needed time to plot the best way to get back down. He hoisted one leg over the beam, levering his body onto the timber joist. He sat down, much to the disappointment of the others watching below.

He looked across the oak beam, inspecting for defects, checking to see how safe he actually was. Like a spotlight the sun's rays hit the inside wall, causing Jack to spot something unusual. He was unable to figure out what it was, so he edged his way along the fragile beam, his legs trembling as he wobbled on the narrow timber joist. Small in comparison to the huge pieces of stone sat a brick, but not your regular, ordinary red house brick.

Imprinted upon the smooth face were two symbols, each within its own circle. They were the two pictures from the coin, one was identical to the England badge and the other was the unusual cross.

"What ya doing?" shouted Holly.

"I think I've found something, it's the pictures from the gold coin," Jack cheered.

If only Jack had some kind of tool to remove the cement. To his surprise, Holly had a Swiss army knife.

Holly's attempt to throw the knife up was terrible. As Jack reached out to catch it, he nearly toppled off. Desperately, he grabbed hold of the beam with his flailing hands, just in time.

Pieces of rubble fell as Jack moved on the timber. Reaching the wall a quivering wreck, Jack leaned against it for support. He hated heights. Why had he allowed Jules to convince him to do this? At least he'd managed to keep hold of the Swiss army knife.

Adrenalin pumped through him as his hand scraped feverishly around the brick, trying to loosen the mortar. The others stood watching, excited. Seconds faded into minutes. His enthusiasm began to wane, the muscles in his arms starting to ache.

Suddenly there was a PING, followed by a grunt. "Have you done it yet? What can you see?" Holly shrilled.

"Um...not exactly... The blade's snapped," Jack mumbled.

"What? My new knife, you've broken it?" Holly hollered.

"Yeah, well it wasn't my fault. This stone stuff is well tough," Jack replied defensively.

The initial ecstasy of unlocked secrets, mountains of gold and treasure maps, gave way to dejection. Everything was going wrong. On top of it all, the gap behind the stone would be too small to hide the treasure behind, he reasoned. It could even be just a random stone used when building the barn.

The chains on the doors started to rattle. A key turned in the padlock. Someone was about to enter the barn.

Before Jack could blink, Martin, followed by Jules, clambered up the old tractor and disappeared through the hole. Jack looked across at Holly who turned and gestured for Jack to hurry up and follow them. Then he, too, vanished through the same exit. For an overweight history geek, Holly could move fast when he needed too.

Jack was all alone, trapped like a pigeon with a lame wing, about to end up in a pigeon pie. (24)

Chapter Nine

FT

Panic flooded over Jack as he desperately tried to think of an escape route. In a flash, he slid down the rope and headed for the hay bales stacked in the corner. Just as the barn doors creaked open flooding the barn with daylight, Jack dove behind the tightly wrapped bales of hay.

"Pesky kids," a deep voice boomed. The methodical sound of the farmer's heavy boots crunching on the ground grew steadily louder. He was heading straight towards Jack.

Jack's heart was beating so loud he was certain it would give him away. The footsteps were getting closer. Jack held his breath. Any second now, he would be...THUD!

Something slammed down directly above him. Bits of straw scattered everywhere as another hay bale was added to the pile. Then, the farmer began to walk away. Phew!

Jack was desperate to find out what lay hidden behind the brick and it felt like an eternity until finally, the doors groaned shut. The bright daylight faded once more as he heard the chains rattle.

Peering from the safety of the hay wall Jack double-checked to see if the coast was clear. More pieces of broken machinery were now stacked against the limp tractor. As Jack turned to climb back up the rope he realised something else had changed. The farmer had cut down the rope.

No rope or ladder meant the end. He scanned around the room for inspiration, desperate for just one useful item. Nothing, except a few lumps of useless metal, the broken feeding trough, the tractor – but that was at the wrong side of the barn – and the stack of straw.

Gutted, Jack reluctantly resigned himself to the fact that he would have to wait for another day.

He stared at the bales of hay... The hay, he could stack them against the wall. Quickly, he rushed over and grabbed hold of one, tugging it with all his might. A few seconds later, Jack was on his back clutching a few pieces of straw in his hands. The bales were too heavy and he had a sore backside to prove it.

The old, rickety trough!

He managed to drag it the short distance and grabbing the trough's metal legs he lift it skywards. Huffing and puffing, Jack pushed it into the air until it was almost vertical. His foot slipped and he lost his balance. The trough was about to tip backwards and with every remaining ounce of energy, he gave it one last almighty push.

Bang! The feeding tray with the rotted hole in its belly clattered against the wall and came to rest in the perfect spot.

Just before he attempted to climb his new improvised ladder, he caught sight of a broken pitchfork. One of its forks bent badly and with a little encouragement wiggling it back and forth, the prong snapped off – he now had an HPD.

Back on the beam with his new Hypertensonic Probing Device – mortar scraping implement for short – in hand, he attacked the wall. The heat beating down on the barn made it feel like the inside of an oven and Jack was the Sunday roast. It was amazing how difficult the old-fashioned cement was to scrape away, even with the HPD.

He toiled away until finally, he felt the brick loosen. Jamming the HPD in the gap where the mortar used to be, he levied the stone brick. It began to move.

Jack could not stop his hands from shaking as he freed the stone from its resting place. He put the stone down on the beam and peered inside the hole. It was too dusty to see clearly. Allowing the dust to settle he peered in again. To his surprise, it was empty apart from bits of broken mortar.

All his efforts for nothing, gutted!

Chapter Ten

H

Detective Jack was on the hunt and soon found the others at the summerhouse. Not only had they left him to the farmers mercy, they had also eaten all the clotted fudge.

"So you made it out alive then," laughed Martin.

"For your information, I got it," Jack said proudly waving the brick above his head. He proceeded to tell them all about the farmer chopping down the rope and his struggle to find a way back up to the beam.

"Yeah, but what was hidden behind the brick?" Holly mumbled with a mouth full of Cornish fudge. The others looked at Jack eagerly.

Annoyed at them for deserting him, but especially for not saving any of the fudge for him, Jack's grip tightened around the brick.

His friends stared in amazement. A secret compartment clicked open in the back of the stone.

"Hurry up and show us what's inside," urged Martin.

Shell-shocked, Jack pulled out a faded piece of white lace. A bronze-coloured key about sixteen centimetres long fell out of the lace and into his palm. Carved into the oval handle was the same three-lion emblem as the coin. Flipping the key between his fingers, Jack stared at the cross, the same symbol as on the gold coin and, carved into the stone brick. He knew he had stumbled onto something important.

Jack found it hard to imagine that people could produce this level of craftsmanship back in the olden days. Mr. Whitlock, the history teacher with the droning voice to send a glass eye to sleep, had told them all about a period called the Dark Ages. Jack was convinced it referred to a time before light bulbs existed. It was not surprising no one could invent things like computers and mobile phones back then, if it was too dark to see what they were doing.

Wrapped within the lace folds was a piece of yellowing paper. Carefully, he unravelled the parchment. The ink was partially faded, written in unrecognisable words. No matter how long he stared at the letter, he was still unable to understand a single word.

"Well what is it?" asked a voice Jack did not recognise. He looked over to see a smaller kid with jet-black hair, standing there.

"Who's that?" demanded Jack. This was not part of their arrangement.

"He talks funny, don't he?" piped up the strange boy with rat-like features, who appeared younger than the others.

"Who's the joker?" Jack enquired.

"I'm BT and I'm ten," he said proudly, stepping

forward and holding out his hand. Jack refused to shake BT's hand – inviting a ten-year-old was pushing it too far.

BT's real name was Anthony Baker. His dad was some kind of techno-geek-inventor who was always providing his son with the latest hi-tech gadgets. Most of Jack's stuff had to be somebody else's rejects. His friends knew Baker-tech as BT.

"You should've used sticky ladders to climb the wall. That would've been so much easier for you. My dad invented them for NASA as a lightweight replacement for oversized gravity boots in space," BT said proudly.

He shook his head in disbelief at what he was hearing. It would take more than silly inventions to impress Jack. He then made BT swear an oath of silence before properly showing everyone the letter and key he had retrieved from the barn.

Jack was hoping either Jules or Holly would be able to decipher the letter, but they were no help either. Why did people make clues if no one could understand what they meant? Nothing made sense.

Holly had a plan. In town, there was an antiques shop where his uncle, who collected unusual coins, had taken him. Jack did not like the idea, mainly because he had not thought of it.

***

Only a few weeks ago the holidays were looking bleak. The thought of leaving his friends behind and moving house had turned Jack's world into a bowl of miserable soup. He had to admit, living in Barnoldswick was not as bad as he had envisioned.

They stopped off at the local shop. Ice pops all round thanks to BT. He had no intention of saying so, but Jack was inwardly glad BT had come along— he was the only one with any money.

They halted outside a shabby-looking shop window so abruptly that Martin crashed into the back of BT. Jack tried hard to conceal his smirk.

They hesitated for a moment before entering the shop. The shop front was so filthy it was almost impossible to see in. The letters stuck to the frosted glass of the shop door read 'Danny's _ntiques.' A scruffy, rectangular cardboard sign hanging by a piece of string read 'Open.'

A brass bell jingled as Jules pushed the grimy door open. Instantly, a musty smell hit Jack's nostrils. He glanced around to find its origin. The shop was so dark and dingy that it was almost impossible to see anything. This was supposed to be a shop where people bought things!

As Jack tried, in vain, to look beyond the dust covered books which were heaped in piles on tables, chairs, and even the floor – why on earth the owner didn't invest in a bookshelf was beyond him, – his gaze fell upon what, to the untrained eye, appeared to be a glass-topped coffee table.

Rushing hastily towards it, he tripped over a box lying in the middle of the floor. If the bell had not alerted the shop owner to their presence then Jack knocking over half the shop surely would have.

Gutted! He had always wanted a retro, tabletop Space Invaders game and this was the first time he had ever seen one in real life. Before he could check it out, the wooden beaded curtains at the far end of the shop rattled and a large beast of man lumbered through, towards them.

"Can I help you?" the voice almost deafened them. The giant of a man looked tough with his shaven head.

"Hi, Mr. Pullen. It's me, Shaun Hollingsworth. You know my uncle, Simon King," Holly stated in his Sunday best voice.

"Do I?" Danny replied, uninterested.

"Yeah, he gets old coins from you," Holly explained pointing to a tray of coins in a glass counter display.

"Ah, yes, that Simon King." Realisation dawned across the shopkeeper's face. "And what can I do for you lot?" he asked abruptly. "I haven't got all day."

"My mate's got some old key and was hoping you might be able to tell us more about it," replied Holly. Everyone looked at the man eagerly apart from Jules; she was busy checking out all the antiques locked away in the glass cabinet.

"Well let's see it then," the shopkeeper demanded, holding out his enormous paw of a hand.

Jack stepped closer, a faint odour of stale beer wafted over him. He offered the key to Danny – according to the sign on the outside of the shop. Danny rubbed the stubble on his unshaven chin while his eyes rested on the key.

"Mmm," he pondered. "Quite an old key you have here," he said. "The pipe appears pure bronze. And the ward too, must be thirteenth, fourteenth century at least, by the looks of it. Quite remarkable, I've not seen anything like this before. Let me have a closer look then?" he asked wrestling the key from Jack's grasp. Danny's eyes flickered with excitement.

After briefly turning the key over, he handed it back to Jack.

"Oh yes, quite common," he said with an obvious change to his tone of voice. "I've seen plenty of these. Nothing of any interest to me, I'm afraid," he dismissed them. "Well, come on then. Be off with you, I don't have all day. I'm a very busy man," he said ushering them out the door.

The five kids stumbled out of the shop. Echoes of the bell rang in Jack's ears as the door slammed shut behind them. Danny flipped the sign around...he was now closed.

"What was all that about?" Jack wondered aloud.

"It was like he recognised it and was excited. Then he just got rid of us," Martin said.

"So you noticed that as well," Jack added. "What do you reckon, then?"

"Well he's never been like that with my uncle before..." Holly said indignantly.

"Did anyone notice the box in the glass cabinet?" Jules interrupted.

"What box? What's that got to do with anything?" blurted Martin.

"That odd-shaped box," Jules explained. "I'm sure it had the same symbol on as the key,"

"And your point is?" Jack was confused.

"Well that means he's obviously lying. He must know what that symbol represents because he's already seen it on the box."

"Wow sis! That's pure brilliant," admired Martin.

"I tell you what I think," Jack said. "We're still no closer to knowing a single thing."

The small group started to squabble. Nothing was turning out how Jack had pictured.

"The letter!" Jules cheered with excitement, cutting through the disarray.

"Yeah. What about it, Jules?" Jack puzzled.

"It's well old yeah, and in olden times a lot of letters were written in French," she explained.

"But even if it is, none of us can read French," Jack stated, the others gathering closer.

"Yes I know we don't," she replied patiently and slowly, as if talking to a three-year-old. "But I know someone who does. Miss White."

"And who's she when she's at home?" Jack stared at her, still none the wiser.

"Oh I forgot, you've not gone to our school yet. She's the French teacher," Jules clarified.

"Clever... We can't wait for another three weeks until school starts to solve this," Jack stressed.

"But I know where she lives," said Jules, patiently. "It'll only take us about ten minutes to get to her house from here." (12)

Chapter Eleven

E

Jules led them through a narrow snicket hindered by years of untamed growth. The shortcut saved five minutes and time was the one thing they needed.

They were off to Monkroyd, a posh housing estate. Apparently, Jules explained after learning about it at school, it was once the home of some wandering monks, hundreds of years ago. The monks settled down and began to build a monastery only for the inhabitants to run them out of town and so they settled over in Leeds and built Kirkstall Abbey instead.

Jack was impressed at Jules' knowledge. In fact, Jules and Holly between them seemed to know everything. The only subject Jack knew plenty about was football. If listening in class were a subject, it would be his least favourite lesson. He generally found his mind was too busy thinking about other things, like being talent spotted by a scout for the Hammers and then whisked off to their training academy.

"Come on," Jules shouted. "We haven't time for dawdling."

"Fair enuff," huffed Jack.

Jack heard the tinkle of a bell and some kid hurtled past on a bike. Before he had time to see who it was – not that he actually knew any other kids in town – they were long gone. If only he was riding a bike, anything was better than trudging up the steep hill.

"I knew I should have brought my hover scooter," exclaimed BT.

It was a hot day and Jack was desperate for a drink. At first, the thrill of the adventure had been a real high, but he never expected it to be hard work. This was supposed to be fun. "Are we there yet?" he called out.

"Nearly," came the sharp reply.

After what felt more like climbing Mount Everest, they eventually reached the top. The yellow stone houses that were Monkroyd all had neat gardens. In one garden grew a couple of miniature palm trees. Jules stopped outside one of the houses and began waving her arms around frantically. "Okay, I'm coming." Jack wished they would install escalators on steep hills.

Jack's heart raced with the sound of the doorbell. Standing outside the teacher's door was almost unbearable. What if she would not be able to help them, or, worse still, told them it was a hoax letter? They would be right back where they started, still without answers.

There was no reply. The fact that she may not be home had not crossed his mind and looking around at the others, he realised this fact had escaped them too.

"We could wait?" Jules said, disappointed.

"But she could be out for the day," Martin pointed out. "Ha-ha Julie-wulie has dropped a clanger 'cause there's nobody home."

"She could even be on holiday," BT added.

Jack's heart sank at those words. The thought of being so near, yet so far was disheartening; especially after climbing all that way up the huge hill.

Just as the five of them began to squabble over whose fault it was, the sound of a chain jangling stopped them, dead in their tracks.

A woman in her mid-thirties stood before them. She was wearing a long, white towelling dressing gown. Her peroxide blond hair looked as though she had just stuck her fingers in a plug socket. Without any makeup on, she gave the appearance of having just crawled out of bed. It was mid afternoon!

"Er...I'm sorry," Jules stuttered, "I think we've got the wrong house."

"Julie Brown, is that you?"

"Miss White? ... I'm sorry I didn't recognise you."

"Late night ... Anyway, what are you all doing here? How can I help?"

"We've got a note we need translating. I think it's possibly French. Please?" Jack had never heard Jules speak so politely.

"Well I..."

"Please miss, it's really important."

"Well I suppose you'd better all come in then," the teacher said walking into the house, leaving the gang to follow. Jules stepped boldly over the threshold and into the teacher's home. After a slight hesitation, all the boys quickly followed.

They found themselves standing in a large open-plan kitchen/dining area. Dozens of empty beer cans and wine bottles covered the glass dining table and kitchen worktops. There were even a couple of Pringle tubes – cheese and onion, Jack's favourite and he wondered if they were any left in them.

Holly was already munching merrily away. Jack was amazed how Holly managed to find a blueberry muffin and not only that, not share any of it with the rest of them.

Miss. White was already in action, clearing the mess off the table into a black bin bag. With a cloth in one hand and a trigger-spray bottle in the other, the table was soon spotless. It would have been impossible – even for Sherlock Holmes – to deduce what had been there minutes earlier.

As Jack sat down on the plush, cream leather dining chair, Jules' French teacher asked if they wanted drinks and came back armed with five glasses of Coke on a tray.

Jack stared into his glass watching all the bubbles exploding onto the surface of the brown liquid. He often imagined they were tiny little bubble creatures with lives of their own and the gurgle-fizz sound was their way of communicating.

"Urgh," Jack choked, spitting the dark liquid back into his glass – and missing.

"What's wrong?" Jules asked.

"It's been poisoned," Martin shouted.

"That's not Coke," Jack moaned trying to scrape the taste off his tongue.

"Of course not, you Muppet," BT laughed. "It's Dandelion and Burdock."

"Dande-what?"

"Dandelion and burpppp-a-lot," belched Martin.

Just then, Miss. White reappeared armed with her trigger bottle, again. She flashed Jack a disdainful look. Sheepishly he slumped further down in his chair while she cleaned up, for a second time. Jack was relieved the minute the teacher left the kitchen. When the excitement subdued, Miss. White re-entered the kitchen dressed more appropriately for so late in the day.

"So where is this note then?" she enquired.

"Oh right, yeah," Jack unzipped his pocket, carefully pulled out the piece of paper, and gingerly passed the aged parchment to Miss. White. Jack noticed the excitement in her eyes, just like Danny from the antiques shop.

"Wow," she said. "Where did you get this? It is extremely old."

Before Jack could answer, Jules jumped in. "It's his grandad's."

"This is an historical treasure. Look at the mark at the bottom..." Miss. White explained.

He had noticed that mark too, but just thought it was spilt ink.

"It looks like a royal mark," Miss. White continued, peering through a magnifying glass. "Yes it is. Do you know what this is?" she asked excitedly, waving the letter in their faces.

Jack wanted to say to her; 'of course we don't; otherwise we wouldn't have needed to bring it to you in the first place.' He was glad Miss. White could not read his mind.

"If I'm not mistaken, this looks like the mark of King Richard the Second."

"Richard the Lionheart?" Martin asked excitedly. Even Jack had heard of him.

"No silly," Jules interrupted. "That was King Richard the first."

"That's right Julie. Well done," agreed Miss. White.

"So what does it say?" Jack was eager to know.

He watched as she scanned over it. "It's not that easy to interpret."

"But I thought you were the French teacher," Jack continued.

"Yes I am, but this is written in Old French and over six-hundred years old. To be in such pristine condition is quite remarkable. Where did your grandad find it?" she half asked, still busy examining the page.

"It was passed down to him," Jules quickly responded. "Apparently, Jack is related to the royal family."

"This is incredible. It should be in a museum," advised Miss. White.

"But can you translate it?" Martin asked eagerly.

"I think I can translate some of it at least," Miss. White said. The four gathered closer in anticipation. "It begins with something about 'I don't have long left. I fear the wound from the axe will soon finish my path. You must move my body once the soul is released and continue our quest, my secret brethren of the four,' It mentions something else; 'you who represent the four corners, my wealth has been hidden for the good of our cause.'

That is most bizarre. I have never come across anything relating to this before. I am finding it difficult to read the middle of the page. It has faded rather badly but roughly translated it says; 'Baron De Clifford followed the path of God.' There is a space before the final section, which has been written separately. 'The secret to life is at the centre of death. Remember me as you pass by. As you are now so once was I. As I am now so you must be. Therefore prepare to follow me.'"

Silence hovered over the kitchen. It suddenly felt cold considering it was such a warm day. Jack shivered, as if the King's ghost, trapped more than six hundred years, had finally been released.

"Is that it?" Martin broke the silence. "Is there no more? Nothing about buried treasure?"

What a big mouth. Jack knew he should not have trusted them with his secret.

"So this is what it's all about, is it? You've found this in your grandad's house and hoped it was a clue to some hidden treasure?"

Jack looked at the historical note, written over six hundred years ago. Miss. White had placed it on the table and he wondered if she would ever give it back to him. While the others were still talking, his hand slowly crept across the table. Then, in a flash, he retracted his hand, slipping the evidence nonchalantly into his pocket.

"Do you realise," the teacher went on. Jack thought she sounded more like a history teacher. "Many historians report that after King Richard was usurped from the throne in, I think 1398..."

"1399 miss," Holly interrupted.

"Thank you Shaun." Jack grinned. He could sense the teacher less than impressed by Holly's intrusion. "History isn't my strong point... but anyway, apparently he had been struck by an axe. But do you know what they found when they opened his tomb years later?"

"A body?" Jack asked.

"Treasure," Martin blurted excitedly.

"A mummy," BT added.

"Historical artefacts," mumbled Holly, still munching on his muffin.

"Nothing," said Jules. Trust a girl to give such a boring answer.

"Well, yes and no," Miss. White answered. "They found a body, but with no evidence of any head wound—which means according to this—they must have switched his body. This note was to his fellow members of some secret order, telling them to move his remains and use his fortune to further their cause. It's astonishing, a fantastic discovery indeed!"

Jack was amazed Miss. White had managed to decipher all that from the letter.

If someone had moved the king's body in secret, then they could have moved his treasure too. This was what they were now after. King Richard the Second had left clues, pointers to the whereabouts of his secret resting place.

Jack and his friends were closing in! (13)

Chapter Twelve

K

Jack lay on his bed thinking about the key and the ancient letter. It was over six-hundred-years-old! Finding the treasure would be bigger than West Ham winning the Premiership, for sure.

He figured he could spend the rest of his life looking for the treasure – never to find it, just like his grandad. Why did the king have to make this so complicated? He could have just said; 'X marks the spot under the fifth oak tree,' or something similar.

He looked at the coin studying it carefully. He spun it around in his fingers, showing the three lions on one side and the cross on the other.

As he held it up to the light, he noticed for the first time a pair of hands cupped together. Excitement coursed through his veins. There were four of them altogether, one in each corner.

"The Four Corners," he shouted in triumph.

His mind remembered the letter. Miss. White had mentioned the Secret Society of the Four Corners. This proved the letter was real and the letter proved the coin was real.

Jack pulled the letter out of his pocket. There they were again in each corner. The four corners – a perfect match. He was dying to tell the others about it in the morning.

The making of new friends: Jules, Holly, BT and Martin had quickly replaced the upset of leaving his old friends behind. Even his grandad was cool. On top of that, he was involved in the adventure of a lifetime in search of an ancient King's treasure. Even if they never found it, he would remember this summer forever!

He fell asleep with a smile on his face.

***

Jack awoke in darkness, holding his breath. He was certain someone, or something was in his room. Had he been dreaming or had something awakened him? He was positive he had gone to sleep with his light still on. An ethereal light glowed in the corner of his room. He was sure he heard one of his drawers sliding open.

"Mer-mum, is that you?" Jack stammered.

The light instantly vanished. An icy blast of cold air caused him to shiver.

The old man's ghost!

He knew ghosts were afraid of the light. His trembling hand edged closer to his bedside lamp, his one chance to scare it away. Jack flicked the switch on.

The curtains were fluttering in the night breeze testament to the fact his window had been opened. He jumped up and ran across the room, straight past the open window, through the door and across the landing.

"Mum... dad," Jack shouted. "The ghost was in my bedroom!"

After explaining what had happened at least five times, he was ushered back to bed and assured everything was fine. He was not happy; there was definitely something in his room.

All the drawers were open. Clothes thrown all over his bedroom floor. Even books and toys were scattered everywhere. "I suppose I made all this mess, as well? I was only dreaming, was I? And how did the light turn itself off?" he complained, storming into his room.

***

Jack awoke to the sound of the radio. Then he remembered what happened in the night, a visit from the ghost of the old man, forcing him to go back to sleep with every electrical item he possessed, switched on.

That morning Jack got dressed in the bathroom.

Soon, he was in the summerhouse with the others. They stared in disbelief as Jack told his story about the phantom visitor. Martin hid behind a cushion, but Jules did not believe in ghosts. Jack tried to convince them he was telling the truth.

"Did you bring the letter with you?" asked Holly.

It seemed he was not remotely interested in Jack's near-death experience. All Holly was bothered about was history. Jack failed to understand what kid in his right mind could love history that much.

"It's at home," Jack replied.

"We could have a look at finding something about 'The Four Corners' on the Internet. I've got loads of websites saved in my favourites that deal with historical artefacts and images, you know," Holly told them.

"What a great idea," said Jules.

"Doesn't anyone believe me?" Jack complained.

A minute later, the five of them were charging through Jack's garden gate, towards the front door.

"Look...footprints!" Jules' shouted, pointing to the flowerbed below the front window.

They all crowded in front of the window. Sure enough, there in the ground were about half a dozen marks left by a large shoe. Jack's bedroom window was directly above.

"Do you know what this means?" Jules asked.

Jack just shrugged his shoulders.

"It couldn't have been a ghost in your room because ghosts don't leave footprints. You had a burglar!"

The cogs in Jack's brain began to whir into action. If there had been a burglar, why would they want to steal anything from him? He did not possess anything worth stealing.

"What if they were after the letter?" BT suggested.

It sounded feasible, thought Jack. For once BT had said something useful. "But who would be after that old letter? No one knows about it except us and... your <u>French teacher</u>."

Jack's hand shot to his open mouth in disbelief.

"Well I bet she's after it," Martin joined in. "I bet she read a clue in the letter about the hidden gold and made up a load of rubbish to throw us off the scent."

"Of course, it all makes sense," stated Jack. He was convinced Miss. White had done it.

"But there's just one problem with your theory. Miss. White has small feet. These prints are way too big to be hers," Jules pointed out.

Jules was right – yet again. Deep down, Jack knew Miss. White had been his late-night visitor. Now, he just had to prove it.

A light bulb pinged in his brain.

"But it was her. Don't you see? She wore someone else's shoes, which were far too big for her. So if anyone found her tracks, they would think it was a man." Jack had cracked the case wide open and stood back as the others nodded in approval. It felt good to be so right.

"Anyway, come on. We need to make sure the note's safe," Jack announced before turning on his heel and heading towards the front door. The others decided they would rather stay outside. Although it turned out there was no ghost, the others erred on the side of caution.

As soon as Jack flung the front door open, he heard his mother call him into the living room.

"Can't it wait? I'm busy," he replied, but his mother insisted.

To his surprise, a man in a dark brown suit sat in the living room drinking out of one of his mum's best china teacups. Jack eyed him up and down. He must have been in his forties with thick, dark hair, slicked back with a whole tub of grease. As the man put the dainty china cup up to his lips and took a sip, Jack noticed he wore a huge gold sovereign ring.

"So you're the juvenile rascal, then?" the stranger spoke. "Been out making mischief with your little chummies, have you?" the man continued.

"Er...yeah, I mean no," Jack mumbled.

'What's with the questions and who is he?' Jack wondered.

"This is Inspector Tyrrell," his mum answered as though she had just read his mind.

"Please, call me David," the man interrupted.

"He's come about the break-in last night."

"Eh, but I thought you didn't believe me?"

"Of course we did luvvie, but we didn't want to give you nightmares. And besides, the small window near the back door has been smashed."

"So do you mind if I ask you a few questions?"

Inspector Tyrrell asked, flipping open a notepad, while pulling a pen out of his top pocket and yet somehow managing to balance the china cup, all at the same time. "Why do you think they specifically targeted your room?"

"I don't know."

"I see," Inspector Tyrrell said and began to scribble something down. "Have you noticed anybody unusual loitering nearby recently?"

"I'm not sure."

"Mmm. Have you found anything that may be valuable recently?"

"Erm, not really," Jack was getting bored. Interrogation was not enjoyable. If only he could think of an excuse to get out of the room – and fast.

"You're not a very talkative young chappy are you?"

"That's 'cause I don't know anything. Can I go now mum? My friends are waiting for me outside." Jack jumped out of his seat hoping she would see how desperate his need to leave the room was.

"It's okay Mrs. Hunter, I've finished with him, <u>for now</u>."

Jack quickly left the room and charged upstairs. He clambered onto his bed and perched on the edge. He was not quite tall enough to see on top of the wardrobe.

"<u>Yes</u>, they're still there," he cheered as his fingertips touched the medieval objects.

He shoved the items into his pockets and jumped back down. As he opened his bedroom door, Jack swallowed sharply. Inspector Tyrrell was outside his room.

"Whatcha, fella? In a rush, are we? What are you up to?" he said firing his questions at Jack.

"Er-I-I'm-just. Anyway, what are you doing up here?" Jack asked, suspiciously.

"I'm trying to find the bathroom," replied the man.

"It's that room there," Jack pointed. He ran down stairs two at a time, glad to be away from the police inspector.

Jack stood in the front garden explaining about the stranger in his house. They heard the front door open and out stepped Inspector Tyrrell. Jack watched as the Inspector shook his mum's hand as he left and sauntered down the path, whistling badly. The man paused briefly in front of them.

"Remember Jack; if you recall anything that you think you should tell me, anything at all, then you best get in touch."

A minute later, he climbed into his smart, black, sports car, started the engine, and drove away.

"Who was that?" asked Holly.

"Blimey, he's a bit creepy," Martin shivered.

"Some police guy about last night," Jack said.

Just as Jack was about to take his next step, Jules placed her hand across his chest.

"Stop!"

Before Jack could complain about her silly games – 'stand on a crack, marry a rat.'

"Look. Look at his footprints." On the pale paving slabs of the path was a small puddle.

For a minute, Jack and the others remained speechless. He stared at the damp mark left by the man's shoe. It looked identical to the one left in the soil by the burglar.

BT jumped straight in with the opportunity to impress with his latest gadget.

Seconds later...

"I've measured the footprint in the soil with my infrared measuring device," BT explained, placing his wrist next to the print on the path. "Keeping in mind the edges of the print will have evaporated, a slight recalculation, a little calibration...here," the rest looked on whilst he pressed a few buttons on his slim-line watch. "Yes, it's the same width, length and pressure, with an equal spacing of the tread marks," BT announced triumphantly.

"Wow! That gizmo tells you all that?" Jack was mightily impressed. "What else does it do?"

"Well it's got the latest deep-sea, underwater technology along with a built-in electronic mass converter," BT explained.

"What he means is that it does everything, except tell the time," Martin joked.

"Actually, it also carries a stun dart with the

poison of a South Chilean red-back spider. It's powerful enough to kill a rabbit. But I'm not sure about bigger subjects. I've yet to test it out," BT continued, staring straight at Martin looking deadly serious. Jack thought he heard a faint gulp coming from Martin's direction.

"So if he is the man who broke into my house last night, he must have been sent by Miss. White," concluded Jack, still trying to prove his theory.

"But why would some copper be working for her?" BT wondered.

"And another thing," Jules pointed out. "Those regulation shoes that the police wear have air cushioned soles just like Dr. Martens."

"And your point is?" asked Jack abruptly.

"You see loads of people with them on. So it could have been someone else is all I'm saying."

"But how come some police guy can afford to be driving around in a brand new Jag? He's gotta be a crook," BT pointed out.

"But Miss. White just doesn't seem the type to be working with crooked cops," Holly reasoned.

"That's right," said Jack. "It has to be the teacher. He could be her boyfriend or sommat."

"There is another theory," Jules added. "It could've been Danny from the antiques shop."

As everyone thought about who the culprit might be, Holly remembered. "But I don't recall us showing Danny the letter?"

"But it might not have been the note they were after. We just assumed that. It could've been the key," Jules drove across her point.

"That's right," Martin joined in. "Did you see the way Danny reacted when he saw the key?"

"Of course." Jack did remember.

"So, what are we going to do about it? Tell your parents? I think we should go to the cops." Jules said in her typical no-adventure fashion.

"No," Jack blurted out, "they'll never believe us. My mum and dad didn't even believe me about someone breaking into my room last night until they found the broken window. They said I was just having a nightmare. And we can't go to the cops in case that Inspector is the burglar. No, we have to do this. But now we know someone is onto us, we need to act... and quick."(23)

Chapter Thirteen

IN

"I've had an idea," Holly announced. "In the letter, Miss. White read something about a Baron De Clifford."

"And... your point is?" asked Jack.

"Skipton Castle was built in 1090 by Robert de Romille, a Norman Baron. Well, in fact, the original castle was more like a timber fort. A Robert Clifford started the beginnings of the stone castle that you can still see today in the early fourteenth century. Without checking I'm not sure if he was a Baron, but he was living around the same time of King Richard the Second."

"So that means they could have been bezzy mates?" said Martin.

"Yeah... and the King could have gotten the Clifford guy to hide the treasure in his castle. I mean what better place to stash your gold where no one can get to it than a castle with battlements and knights?" Jack had never heard of Skipton Castle but it sounded cool and a good place to start.

Jack pictured himself dressed in a suit of armour, laying siege to the castle with his friends. After defeating a monstrous fire-breathing dragon, he would find a secret passageway that would lead to mountains of gold and priceless jewels.

"...but how are we gonna get there?" Jack heard Martin ask.

"We could blag my uncle to take us. We'd all easily fit into his new Landrover," said Holly.

"No!" shouted Jack. "We can't have any grownups knowing what we're up to. This is <u>our</u> treasure."

"Geeze, you're so paranoid. We don't have to, do we? All we need to do is say it's for class research or something, like a history project," Jules smooth reply resolved the issue.

"Right, that's settled then. Let's meet at my house in half an hour," Holly announced. "And we can go to the sweet shop before we set off."

***

Jack sat in the back of the seven-seater Landrover nursing a fat lip while the others looked to have fared no better.

"Why can't Stoneman just pick on someone else," moaned Martin whose bright red ear was generating enough heat to fry an egg.

The Stoneman had ambushed them on the way to the shop.

"It could have been-mmm-worse," mumbled Holly munching on yet another snack, sporting a bruise on his left cheek. "At least he jumped us before we bought the sweets!"

"Is that all you ever think about?" Jack complained.

"Sweets provide glucose utilization which enhances the brain's energy consumption." Holly proclaimed, leaving Jack speechless.

"Well, he won't have long to go before he's taken away," Jules added.

"What do you mean, 'taken away'?" asked an intrigued Holly.

"The Bully Hunters...Don't tell me you've never heard of them. They are from another dimension but come to our world and take bullies away when they reach sixteen. You've never read about them?" asked Jules in disbelief.

"Of course not. I've never heard so much twaddle before. If it's not of historical or geographical importance, then I won't have read it," replied Holly, calmly.

"Anyway, BT, why didn't you shoot him with your poison dart?" Martin wondered.

"Because I'm not wearing that watch today, I'm wearing my new iWatch," BT said proudly waving his wrist in the air so none of them would miss it.

"There's no such thing," Jack retorted.

"Well there is now. It's a prototype they've given my dad to trial. It's all very hush-hush."

***

Simon dropped them off and arranged to meet them in a couple of hours—much to Jack's relief. He thought Simon was cool, as far as adults go. Yet, no matter how nice he was, he was still a grownup.

They sauntered along the main high street, past all the market stalls selling anything from cheap CDs and sweets to an array of every coloured sock imaginable and, an even greater selection of cheeses. Jack would have never believed so many cheeses existed in the world.

The castle stood at the far end of the high street. Jack was looking forward to seeing a huge, towering fortress at the top of a hill surrounded by a moat. He was disappointed; it was definitely a castle, but rather small and in the middle of town.

To its left was an old church. This held little interest for Jack although Holly found it riveting.

A short cobbled walkway led to the Castle, with two cannons guarding either side of the entrance. Martin sat on one of them and persuaded BT to take a picture of him on his phone. At the main entrance, two stone, twin towers bridged to form an archway.

On the other side of the gateway stood a woman dressed in a long, period coat, obviously pretending to be from that time period. The woman was helpful and Jack decided she did not look too silly after all.

Inside the grounds, they all made a beeline to where the woman had directed them. The right-hand side of the castle was obviously much newer, possibly Tudor. It seemed bizarre saying that something a few hundred years old – was too new.

Jack knew the treasure was here. His family had had plenty of problems and financial bereavements over the years. Now he, Jack Hunter, had the chance to address the balance and halt the tide of the Hunter's misfortune.

They had decided to split up. Jack ran through a doorway and found himself standing in a banqueting hall—according to the guide pamphlet after finally consulting it. 'This great hall would be used for every gathering of the Castle garrison...' he read. It still did not help.

A couple of hours later, tired and hungry, Jack met up with the others. They had checked watchtowers, kitchens, stone stairways, literally dozens of rooms.

Martin claimed to have been in the dungeon. However, no one else had seen it and even the guide pamphlet made no reference to one. To Martin's annoyance, everyone thought he was playing tricks, as usual.

Jack learned Mary Queen of Scots had been held prisoner at the castle. It came as no surprise that Holly already knew this.

Today had promised so much and yet delivered so little, Jack thought. He stepped through the castle's exit wearily scuffing his feet across the cobbles as he admitted defeat. He looked up in time to spot Holly entering the church grounds by the side of the castle. All Jack wanted to do was go home, not go wandering around in old churches.

"Here, you lot. Check this out," Holly pointed to the pavement excitedly.

To Jack they looked just like regular paving slabs as you would find on most streets.

"Do you remember what the teacher told us about what was written in the letter?" Holly asked. Jack was in no mood for games. "She mentioned that King Richard had said about 'Baron De Clifford followed the path of God.'"

"Which means what?" Jack interrupted.

"Well don't you get it? Look at the floor, the path is made up of gravestones."

Squatting down Jack could just about make out some faint writing cut into the stone slab.

"Yes, I get it," said Jules. Jack still failed to see Holly's point, but decided not to ask any more questions. "This path from the castle leads to the church, so it's leading people towards God... the path of God."

"And that means that one of these gravestones could be the resting place of the Baron. We need to spread out and look for the Baron's name written into one of these tombstones," organised Holly.

They were off running up and down the path like five excited puppies. Holly's explanation made it sound as easy as eating chocolate ice cream, but most of the writing had faded, worn away with thousands of tourists walking along the path every year.

"I've found it!" BT suddenly shouted.

Jack was glad, but at the same time secretly gutted, he was not the first to have found it. As they crowded around the grave flagstone, Jack knew it must be a secret door, with a medieval hinge.

"It's the Baron's, alright," confirmed Holly who paused to take a bite out of something he had hidden away in his pocket. "But it's nearly all worn away. Even if there had been a clue, you can hardly read anything."

"Well I'm going to take a rubbing of it anyway, just in case," said Jules, pulling out a pencil and a few pieces of A4 from her shoulder bag. Jack could not believe someone would carry around a pencil and sheets of paper in her bag.

It did not matter now; Jack knew they were never going to find the pot of gold at the end of a rainbow.

Chapter Fourteen

G

The next day Jack felt hollow. The only legible words from Jules rubbings were 'Baron De Town'. All this told Jack was there were many barons riding around in the Middle Ages.

Jules' suggested going back to the antiques shop to take a closer look at the box she had spotted in the glass cabinet. They arrived at the shop just as it started to rain.

"You go in. I won't be a minute. It's my mum," Jules explained as she answered her mobile phone.

The others entered the dingy shop. The jangling bell would have alerted Danny of their arrival like a primitive early warning device. This time Jack wanted to check out the tabletop space invaders game.

He saw a small trunk on top of a pile of wooden boxes. A light ignited in the back of his mind.

'The chest in Grandad's bedroom.' Jack knew there must be more to his grandad's story.

Before he reached the retro game, Jack heard someone shout. Spinning around faster than a Tasmanian devil, Jack saw something that took him by surprise. The Stoneman had appeared from behind the counter. Not waiting for an invitation for a beating, the others scarpered.

Jack's automatic reaction was to stand and watch

as though he was a spectator at some bully sport amphitheatre. Then he realised The Stoneman had spotted him. Jack darted towards the exit. It was a race against time – either be the first to the door and live, or...

Barely making it through the door alive, Jack kept on running. He could hear The Stoneman's boots thudding behind him on the pavement.

Jack saw BT disappear round a corner. Not knowing the area well enough, he decided to follow.

Running round the corner Jack slammed on the breaks. He had run into a blind alley. BT had vanished without a trace. A solid brick wall taller than a house blocked Jack's escape.

The Stoneman stepped into the alley.

"Jack, Jack."

Jack could not see anyone. "Up here..." he heard BT shout and looked up on top of the high wall.

"How did you get up there?" he asked BT.

"Sticky ladders," replied BT.

"Here," he said, throwing him a small container the size of a toothpaste tube, "you need to put it on the soles of your trainers."

There was no time to read the instructions. Jack unscrewed the cap on the tube and squirted the gloopy, yellow liquid onto the soles of each trainer.

"Hurry up!" BT urged. "The Stoneman's coming."

Jack began to walk, upwards. It felt like he was in a dream, the kind with imaginary special powers. He

was scaling the wall, fifteen feet in the air.
  BT had saved him from The Stoneman.

Chapter Fifteen

I

Jack and BT both arrived back at the summerhouse. Jack was dying to tell everyone how amazing BT had been, their miraculous escape from The Stoneman and that sticky ladders actually existed!

No one could recall what happened in the mayhem at the shop or understand what The Stoneman was doing there.

Jules stumbled through the doors.

"You're nev-er going to be-lieve what I've found out?" she panted.

"You know where the treasure is?" piped Martin.

"Is that all you think about? It's about The Stoneman," she replied.

"What about him?" they all asked at once.

"Do you know what his real name is?"

"Yeah silly," said Martin. "It's The Stoneman. Have you caught sunstroke or what?"

"He's called David Pullen," Jules answered.

"So?" said Jack.

"Danny of Danny's Antiques… is his dad!"

"Soooo," Jack said, thoughtfully, "that would explain why he was at the shop."

"But do you know what else?" Jules said, excitedly. "What does he always wear on his feet?"

"Shoes," Martin replied with a puzzled look.

"Doc' Martens," roared Jack. "Of course, he must have broken into our house. We showed Danny the key, he must have known what it was but wouldn't say. Then he sent his overgrown ape of a son to come and steal it."

"And don't forget, The Stoneman's got big feet…like really big," added Martin.

"Who goes around noticing the size of people's feet?" asked BT.

"What do you mean?" Martin whined. "Anyway, she was the one who noticed what he was wearing on his feet…" Martin pointed accusingly at his sister.

Jack thought both the Brown kids were sort of weird as he walked up the lawn towards Simon King's house. He thought he understood Holly's directions to the toilet. He stepped through the open door and found himself standing in a long hallway.

He had never been in a house this big before. He called out a few times, but there was no reply apart from his voice echoing back.

Trying to figure out which room Holly had said was the toilet Jack noticed a door was open just ahead. He peered inside to find it was just a study with books everywhere and a large map of the world stuck on one wall. He was about to check somewhere else when he heard angry voices. Quickly he ran back into the study as the voices grew louder. Whoever it was stopped right outside the study door. Jack hid behind the desk not daring to breathe.

He realised one of the men was Holly's uncle Simon, but the other man's voice seemed familiar too.

"You'd better keep control of them," the other man shouted.

"I assure you, I will sort it," replied Simon.

"I will get it, no matter what," the stern reply came. "But I'm warning you... I want no interference."

"Are you threatening me in my own house?" countered Simon.

Jack knew where he had heard that voice before. Just then, he heard a shuffle of feet and the voices faded down the hallway.

Jack's heart was pounding. He couldn't wait to tell the others what he had just heard. Danny Pullen was in the house and had just threatened Holly's uncle.

As Jack was running back down the lawn towards the summerhouse, everything dropped into place. His friends would be amazed at what he had just discovered. Holly had said his uncle collected unusual coins. What if Danny had inadvertently sold a coin to Simon similar to the one his grandad had given him, before realising the significance of it? Maybe seeing the same markings on the key made Danny realise everything.

They needed to act fast. It was up to them to find the treasure before the unscrupulous Danny. Jack was bursting with information as he charged into the summerhouse.

Before he could tell the others, he found out he was not the only one to have made an important breakthrough. (24)

Chapter Sixteen

S

"So you're saying that the treasure is buried in Towneley Hall?" Martin said, just as Jack burst into the summerhouse.

Jules had finished the phone call with her mum and then wandered into the shop to find it completely empty. Puzzled and with no explanation to anyone's whereabouts, she'd decided to take a few photos on her phone of the box in the glass cabinet.

After downloading the photographs onto Holly's PC, they discovered that the second symbol on the box was none other than the Towneley family crest.

"Baron De Town from the gravestone in Skipton could actually be referring to 'Baron De Towneley'," Jules explained.

"Yeah, but the problem with that theory is that Towneley is Elizabethan," the ever-know-it-all Holly pointed out.

"So, what does it being Eliza-bean mean?" a confused Jack asked.

"It means that Towneley Hall doesn't fit in with the time frame," Holly explained.

"Towneley Hall? Of course! It all fits in," exclaimed Jules.

"But didn't you hear, Jules? Holly says it's not old enough," Jack said. And Jules was usually the sharp-witted one, he thought.

"But that's where you're wrong. I can't believe that I actually know something Holly doesn't! I need to make a note of this in my diary. The house known today isn't that old. But, one small section of it still remains from the original building built in..."

"The late fourteenth century," Holly finished. "But of course! How could I have been so thick? Apparently a very small section that was built around 1400 still remains," Holly butted in, stealing Jules' thunder.

"You guys are pure genius. I don't get how you know all this stuff?" Jack wish he hadn't asked when he saw Holly's jaw dropping in readiness to reply. "I tell you what: Don't answer," Jack said. Holly closed his mouth in disappointment.

"But where is it? I mean, is it far away?" Jack held his breath in anticipation.

"It's in Burnley," Martin said. "It's sort of not far."

"I'll see if I can get my mum to take us in the morning," enthused Jack.

***

The following morning only Jules turned up at Jack's house. It turned out BT had a dentist's appointment and Holly had been grounded. Martin couldn't be bothered getting up – some lame excuse about not feeling well.

Then his mother hit him with more bad news. The catalytic converter had dropped off the car. Jack couldn't believe it, of all the rotten luck, it had to happen today.

Faced with the dilemma of not being able to go and the thought of Danny Pullen getting there first, Jack thought of a plan. He wasn't known for ingenuity and as Jules pointed out; his plan had flaws, a lot of them!

Without asking, Jules borrowed Martin's bike for Jack. As they cycled to his grandad's house, Jack knew if anyone would be able to help, it would be him.

Convincing his grandad to take them wasn't a problem. The rusting brown car was a wreck. It was twice as old as his mum and dad's car; he had never even heard of a Ford Capri let alone seen one.

Jack had a bad feeling about this and with good cause. Within only a few seconds his grandad managed to mount the kerb and bump into a lamppost. Fortunately he was moving at only three miles an hour. The look on Jules face said it all, but they didn't have an option.

The journey to Burnley passed without any further incidents although it has to be said sixteen pieces of good luck and half a dozen portions of fortune were needed. His grandad steered the car along the country lanes like a weaving bullet.

To help keep his mind off the death-defying journey, Jack suggested playing a game called, Pick the Best Cars. Whoever spotted the most expensive car would be the winner. He thought competing against a girl would be a breeze. Jack was glad when they reached their destination so he didn't have to play anymore. Getting whipped by a girl was becoming habitually annoying.

Jack stepped out of the car happy to stand on solid ground.

Towneley Hall was straight ahead. The stately mansion was all square edges – a complete contrast to Skipton castle with its circular walls and round, tall turrets. A lake—well more like a large pond— sprawled across the lawn in front of the building.

As they walked towards the entrance, an ancient-looking, wizened tree stood randomly in the middle of the courtyard. It was surrounded by a...

"Bed? Did you see that?" Jack laughed.

Jack's grandad paid their admission fees. They started the race against Danny to hunt down the next clue. There were rooms and staircases in every direction.

"I'm sure we've already been down here," Jack groaned.

"I know. It's like a maze. You need a map just to find your way about," Jules replied as the two of them entered a large room together. It looked more like a modern art gallery than a room in a stately home. "This isn't right. We're not going to find anything in here. It's too modern," she agreed.

They sped past all the boring paintings hanging quietly on the walls. The hushed atmosphere made it feel more like a library. People flitted between paintings like honey bees buzzing from flower to flower.

At the far end of the gallery they found an exit that led them into a much smaller room. It contained a dozen or so stuffed animals mounted in glass cases. Jack wanted to stay and look at the two badgers playing together or take a closer look at the stuffed fox bearing its sharp teeth. Even the snowy owl chasing a tiny field mouse looked realistic. But, none of this would help him with their quest.

After rushing down another flight of stairs and through another doorway, they found themselves standing in a long, wood paneled hallway. "Cool! This is well old," said Jack.

"No it's still too new. Well, I mean you're right, it's old, but at a guess, I would say Elizabethan," said Jules.

"I'm sure there must be something in here. It looks old enough to me," believed Jack.

Not wanting to be deterred, Jack looked into one of the bedrooms nearby. "See? Look there above the bed, there's a carved plaque and it's got the three lions' motif on it."

An ornately carved, dark wood four-poster bed sat

all forlorn, almost filling the whole room. A wooden coat of arms hung on the wall directly above the head of the bed. The regal crest was split into four different pictures. One of them was the three lions.

'Jack one; Jules nil,' he told himself.

Much to Jack's dismay, the eagle-eyed Jules pointed out there wasn't a cross or the mark of the four corners to be seen anywhere. The way she was always right wasn't just irritating, it was downright maddening.

After dawdling for longer than necessary in the long gallery, Jack conceded defeat. They doubled back and this time ran down another flight of stairs taking them back to ground level. Once again, they passed through the old kitchen. Suddenly, Jack stopped dead in his tracks, grabbing Jules' arm.

There, on the wall in plain sight, was an old-fashioned safe with writing around a crest of the three lions. But, again, to Jack's frustration, there was no accompanying cross. But there was a key hole. Jack pulled out the old, bronze key he had in his pocket. Before he even placed the key in the lock, he realised his key was way too big for the lock in the safe.

The laborious search dragged on up yet another set of stairs. They passed through a room housing more stuffed animals. This room was dark and gloomy with a dingy smell. One unfortunate creature drew Jack's gaze. It looked like an armadillo.

"Here Jules… look at this strange creature. It says here it's called a pangolin," Jack laughed at the name before reading the rest of the plaque. "The pangolin or 'scaly ant eater' was sent to Towneley by Sir Herbert Wright. The pangolin has a sticky tongue which it uses for catching ants and termites. It can roll into a ball if it is under attack. Pangolins are an endangered species."

"I've never heard of one," Jules replied.

"What? You mean I've found something that you don't know anything about!" Jack laughed again. "What a weird creature. Well I wouldn't want one of those running around in my garden."

They quickly passed through an area with a real mummy which gave Jack the shivers, before stopping in a room that contained lots of war memorabilia.

"Here, look at this, Jules. This local hero is called Walter Green."

"Who's Walter Green?"

"That's my grandad's name. Well, the Green bit anyway. I wonder if I'm related?"

Jack pictured his grandad as a super-war hero while they dashed into another room, this time decorated in a different theme. Impressive ivories occupied the glass cases. Someone had even carved intricate chess pieces out of ivory. It was all fascinating but, still no hint of a clue.

They wandered back down another staircase to find themselves standing in the stone-flagged reception area, right back where they had started.

That morning, Jack had hoped to find the treasure. Just one tiny clue would be better than nothing at all. He hated defeat. Jack felt compelled to fall back on plan 'B', when stuck and with no other option available… ask Jules!

"Um, I don't know." Jules replied. Jack knew if anyone would be able to pluck an idea out of thin air, it would be her. And if she couldn't help, then that was it, finito.

"Hang on, I won't be a minute," she said and off she dashed.

A moment later, she came hurtling back across the stone floor, her shoes clapping as she ran towards him. Without an explanation, she grabbed hold of his hand and dragged him across the brightly-lit entrance foyer and through a tall archway. Finally, she let go of his hand.

A red velvet, rope barrier was placed across the entrance to stop people from entering into the room. Rows and rows of red chairs were neatly laid out ready for an event. The high ceiling and tall windows allowed plenty of light to flood into the room.

"Well, this doesn't look any good. What did you drag me here for?" asked Jack.

"I asked the curator which part of the house was built in the fourteenth century." Jules pointed to a section of wall with a grand fire surround in the centre. "Apparently, that part of the room is the only bit left inside and then outside there's a small door."

"Door? Well what are we waiting for? I bet that's it…" Jack sprinted off outside with Jules lagging behind.

Five minutes later, they were standing in the exact same spot, again.

"Well, that was a waste of time. I really thought this key might have unlocked the door or at least somethi…"

"Jack. Look, over on the fireplace." Jules whispered excitedly. Jack spun around to see where she was pointing. "Look at the fireplace. It's got the motifs in the two top corners."

Jack stared at the dappled green fire surround. Sure enough, carved into the top left hand corner was the round symbol of the three lions. He felt a tinge of excitement. But, he had been disappointed enough times already today. He tried hard to quell his feeling of jubilation. Slowly, his eyes wandered across to the other corner. The speckled effect of the marble made it almost impossible to spot the cross of the four corners carved into the top right hand corner.

"But what should we do?" he asked her. "We're not allowed in this room."

"We can't let that stupid bit of rope stop us. You go and I'll keep watch," said Jules.

'What, Jules suggesting he broke the rules?' Jack hesitated, trying to weigh the pros and cons. Before he could reach a decision, Jules gave him a push. He stumbled nearly toppling onto the rope. The only way to gain his balance was to lift his leg over it. He now stood in the restricted area.

"Go on before someone comes," Jules urged him.

He scuttled over to the fire, knelt beside it and began examining all around.

"Well?" Jules called over. Jack just shrugged his shoulders. He couldn't see a keyhole anywhere.

Leaning on the fire place to think, he placed his hand on the image of the three lions. Jack heard a click.

Jack was sure he heard footsteps crossing the hallway towards them. He looked up to see Jules waving her arms in desperation. The footsteps were getting louder.

Jules frantically kept looking back and forth between Jack and the person crossing the hallway – like watching a ball being smashed back and forth over a tennis net. She needed to think fast, come up with a plan. Before she could move, the woman in her curator's uniform called out to her, asking if she was alright. For a split second, Jules was caught off guard and before she could react, the woman was upon her.

There was nowhere for Jack to hide in the room and Jules turned expecting to see him caught like a deer in a pair of headlights. As she glanced into the room, she was momentarily stunned.

"Are you alright, darling?" the woman asked again.

Jack had vanished! Jules was busily eyeing every corner, every single inch of the room. She couldn't see him anywhere.

Jack tried to suppress the urge to cough as he inhaled the centuries old dust he had disturbed. Wherever he found himself now squatting, it was pitch black. One minute he had pressed the two symbols on the fire surround, the next he was here. It was as though the wall had reached out and sucked him in.

He wanted to get excited but, it was difficult in the dark and dirty confines. And then he remembered the gift his grandad had given him. He rummaged through his pockets for the key ring with the torch attached to it.

It was hard to see what he was doing and needed another torch just to turn it on. As he gave it a twist, a small blue-white light shone out.

As he looked around Jack realised he had discovered a secret passageway, although he was too tall to stand fully upright in it.

With grim determination, he started to shuffle on his hands and knees, stopping periodically to point the torch. Soon he came to the end of the tunnel. With the small light in one hand, he used his other hand to grope along the sides of the dry, dusty walls covered in cobwebs.

It was a dead end.

Just as he was about to turn around in dismay, his knee banged against something hard. He grimaced in pain, but managed to stave off a yelp. He groped with his hand to pick up the offending object and throw it away in anger. To his surprise, it wasn't a stone. He quickly flashed the tiny beam of light where he knelt. With his knee he had struck what looked to be a metal handle in the floor.

Jack had found a trap door. (12)

Chapter Seventeen

HI

Jack hated the dark. Life would be so much easier if people hid treasure in bright, safe places! He pointed the small beam of light into the black void that lay hidden underneath the trap door.

It was empty. Jack sighed.

It seemed pointless building a secret passageway to hide nothing. Unless... Danny had already found the tunnel!

He spotted a keyhole almost hidden by spider silk in the side of one of the walls.

'Of course, the key,' he shouted in his head. He fumbled in his jeans pocket until his fingers touched the cold, hard metal.

Shaking from a mixture of cold and nerves, he put the key in the web-covered lock, it slipped effortlessly into the opening. Now Jack had reason to be optimistic. He turned the key anticlockwise a quarter turn until he heard a click. His heart jumped, but nothing happened.

He decided to turn the key clockwise, back to its starting position to try again, only he overshot the starting point. CLICK!

The sound boomed so loud in the quiet space that its echo made Jack jump. He flashed the light into the hole. The square hole was about as deep as his forearm. One of the sidewalls had dropped forward revealing a hidden alcove. There was something inside.

His heart skipped a beat as he pulled out a wooden box. He knew time was running out, he quickly tucked his newfound prize against his tee shirt to keep it safe before zipping his hoody back up. He was eager to get back and show Jules what he had found. With the precious object safe, Jack began retracing his steps.

Quick as a jackrabbit he shuffled back along the tiny passageway. Luckily for Jack he was only small. It would be an extremely tight squeeze for an adult to fit through the narrow passage.

A tiny ray of light filtered from behind the fireplace. He paused long enough to remember the symbols carved into the ornate fireplace. He pressed the image of the three lions first – just as he had done before – and then the one with the cross.

***

Jules was pacing up and down, whispering Jack's name while trying to act casual. It felt she had been alone for fifteen hours, not fifteen minutes. She was busy staring at an elderly man leaning heavily on his walking stick. Minutes earlier, the man had been beside Jules, telling her in depth about visiting almost every relic in the country. Just as he turned the corner, she heard a thud and a clattering of chairs coming from within the room.

Jules saw Jack sprawled out on the floor surrounded by a small cloud of dust – as if a bomb had just exploded. Uninterested in the mess, she just wanted to know where he had been hiding?

Sprightly stilettos teetering across the wooden floor in the distance were growing louder.

"Jack, Jack, hurry up. There's someone coming."

***

Jack sat dazed. Had that just happened or was his mind playing tricks? His knuckles were almost white as they gripped the ancient box tightly.

He picked himself up and began dusting himself down; making sure the hidden box was still safe.

The sound of footsteps approaching flagged up a warning. He wasn't supposed to be in there and it was time to move to Defcon 3. Jumping to his feet, he ran across the room nimbly sidestepping a row of chairs, towards the open doorway where Jules stood waving her arms at him.

In one swift, fluid movement, Jack hurdled over the velvet barrier to freedom. A huge sigh of relief washed over him as his ordeal was finally over.

"Jack Anthony Hunter," he heard a voice say.

Jack's heart missed a full beat. Not only was he shocked by the sound of his mum's voice, she had also used his middle name, meaning he was in serious trouble.

Jack passed the box to Jules to hide it from his mum.

"Look at the state of you and where on earth have you been? I've been looking everywhere for you."

Jack tried to block the view from her, but was too late. She pushed him to one side and looked straight into the room that Jack had single-handed turned into a warzone.

Jack braced himself. "Did you do that?" she hollered, every word echoing through the old mansion reverberating off the towering walls, magnified like some form of supersonic wave. Every part of Jack's anatomy shrank inwards. He feared the worst.

"And what do you think you're playing at dragging your grandad along?"

"But I..."

"You know he's not been well."

"No I didn't..."

"I'll have no back-chat. You know full well he's not fit to drive. His tablets cause drowsiness."

"It wasn't my..."

"You should be ashamed of yourself!"

That explained his grandad's terrible driving Jack thought while his mum continued to rant on.

"I'm sorry son," his grandad whispered to him while his mum was busy talking to Jules. "When she found out I wasn't home, she rang and forced it out of me. She can be very persuasive your mother."

It turned out the moment his mum had found out they had convinced grandad into taking them, she had come to Burnley on the first available bus. His mum was a terrible driver and the thought of her behind the wheel of the old sports car caused Jack to predict a return journey fraught with more danger than with his grandad driving.

There was a gloomy atmosphere in the car on the journey home, while his mum was busy driving; Jules and Jack managed a sneaky look at the box.

Jack slipped the box back under his top as they arrived home. His mother stopped the car without killing the engine and ordered Jack inside the house.

"What do you mean?" Jack replied.

"I'm taking your grandad back home. That's what I mean."

"But I need to come too because we've left both bikes there," he pleaded.

"You can get that tomorrow. I want you to go to your room right now. Julie is welcome to come with me and get her own bike."

Jules looked across at Jack as if to say, 'she was sorry.' He understood she had to get her bike; it was as simple as that. Jack slammed the car door and stormed towards the house. (9)

Chapter Eighteen

D

Jack had nearly closed the front door when someone called.

"Ah, you have returned, young Hunter."

The greasy-haired Inspector was just getting out of his flash motor. A shrill bleep sounded as he pressed his key-fob, turning the car's alarm on. Jack didn't like the man and wouldn't trust him, even if his life depended upon it. He would have liked to have told him too, but he was already in enough trouble.

"I was wondering if I could have a few words."

"My mum's not in," Jack said.

Inspector Tyrrell pushed open the garden gate and was halfway down the path. "Well, it's actually <u>you</u> I would like to speak to."

Jack still had the box he had discovered at Towneley Hall hidden safely underneath his tracky top. He folded his arms over the square-shaped bump in an attempt to conceal it from the Inspector's prying eyes. The gut instinct he got every time he saw the Inspector convinced Jack he was the burglar.

"It's about your key," he added.

Jack gulped so loudly that he was certain he would be heard. Jack thought he was prepared for any question, but this took him totally by surprise. "You took a very old and valuable key to a Mr. Pullen who owns the antique shop on the high street. Is this correct?"

"Well sort of," were the first words that came out of Jack's mouth. They weren't the words his brain had sent to his tongue. He had told himself to tell the copper to go away and leave him alone.

"What do you mean by 'sort of'? You either did or you didn't."

"Well we did take a key, but it's not mine," Jack half explained.

"Well whose key is it?"

"I don't know."

"What do you mean you don't know?" Jack sensed Inspector Tyrrell was sounding irritable.

"Well we sort of found it, so we don't know who it belongs too," Jack explained calmly.

"Well why didn't you… oh never mind that. What I want to know is: Where is it now?"

"Why?"

"Because it is important to the case."

"But why?" Jack asked again.

'Why' is a child's secret weapon against prying adults and parents, that is according to some old Greek man called Nostradamus, or was it Eureka? Anyway Jack remembered reading about how it had been invented to defeat an invading army. The two warring kings settled on a battle of wits.

One sent his wisest and most trusted aid while the other sent just a boy. The boy finally defeated the wise man by inventing the question 'why'.

The man had no answer to the never-ending question. And so the legend had been passed down from generation to generation of kids.

"Because... Oh, it doesn't matter. I will come back when your mother gets home. Maybe then I can get some sense out of you."

'Finally,' Jack muttered.

"What is that you've got there?" Inspector Tyrrell pointed towards Jack's jacket just as he was about to leave. A sudden change in his expression gave Jack the impression he already knew the answer.

Jack looked down at his tracky to discover, to his dismay, that half the new-found wooden box was peeking out.

"N-nothing," he stammered. "Anyway, I've gotta go now."

He slammed the door shut before collapsing against the wall. That was a close shave!

He was convinced the policeman was up to something dodgy, but had no way of proving anything.

Jack hid the wooden box in his bedroom. If anyone attempted to burgle them again, no one would think to look inside his pajamas. He also sealed the drawer with his secret spy lock. The box was well and truly secure.

***

At last he had finished the extra chores he had been given in punishment for getting his grandad to drive them to Towneley Hall. He didn't believe how much hard work, cleaning the house could be.

An itch on his head reminded him of the torture his mum had inflicted the previous afternoon. She had returned from his grandad's with a pair of hair clippers. A grade two later, Jack looked ready for military service.

He glanced at the clock: 11:30.

"Is that the time?" he gasped.

He was supposed to be meeting up with his friends. They had loads to discuss about the treasure and the box and Inspector Tyrrell the dodgy policeman. And that was just for starters.

Jack went through the Brown's garden – the shortcut to Holly's uncle's house. Only, he couldn't tell which tree to pass through and ended up walking into a fence post.

Still rubbing his left ear, he found his four friends lounging on the lawn in front of the summerhouse.

"Where've you been?" shouted BT. "I wanted to show you my new pogo-rocket."

"What's up with your face," Jules gasped. "Looks like half of you has turned into a tomato."

"Never mind his face! Look at his head," Martin roared before bursting into song.

"Skin head, skin head over there.
What's it like to have no hair?
Be it hot or be it cold.
I don't know because I'm not bald."

"Shut up," Jack warned. "My mum made me. Anyway, it'll grow back before school."

"Fat chance of that," laughed Martin. "School's only a week away."

Jack sighed. It was daunting enough thinking about going to a new school where Martin, Holly, and Jules would be the only people he knew without facing his first day sporting a skinhead haircut!

"Anyway, Jack, you'll never guess what I've found out!" said Holly.

Holly's words set Jack's heart racing with the hope of a new discovery about the treasure.

"Well," continued Holly, "This morning I was reading through the weekly edition of, The West Craven Chronicle. But you'll never guess what was in it?"

"I don't know," said Jack.

"I should have said, guess what wasn't reported in the newspaper…your house being burgled?" Holly announced.

"And why is that such a big deal?" asked Jack.

"There was nothing in it at all. It should have easily made the front page because it's the only exciting thing to have happened here in weeks.

Instead, the front page was about some seventy-year old and his prize cucumber."

Jack looked at him, still puzzled. He grasped the fact Holly was saying something important, but couldn't understand the relevance. Jules, quick-witted as ever, did.

"Of course!" she said. "This proves there is something a bit weird going on, otherwise, the press would have been all over it. Every week they get tipped off by the police on the local incidents, like cats stuck in trees, kids being rowdy in the park, or robberies."

"So, you think the policeman didn't report it on purpose?"

"I'm not sure, but what I'm saying is this: The fact it's not been reported in here proves that someone with authority has been able to hush this up. This is serious stuff," Jules said, waving the newspaper in front of their faces. A hive of excited chatter broke out.

"Anyway Jack," BT interrupted. "Jules was telling us about a cool box you found in the secret tunnel. Have you got it with you?"

"No, I left it at home, but I can go and get it," Jack offered.

"Yeah, 'cause I want to find out more," Holly added. "If someone really high up and important is in on all this, I want to solve it before they do." (13)

Chapter Nineteen

D

Jack ran home to get the box. Everything was turning out perfectly and with history wizard Holly on his side, the bad guys wouldn't stand a chance.

He returned home to find the front door partly open. "Mum," Jack called with no response. He tried calling again upstairs, but still no reply. Jack had a strange feeling about this and rushed into his bedroom, to where he had set up the hair trap.

Jack remembered his conversation with BT clearly.

'What you've never heard of the hair trap?' BT had sounded surprised.

BT seemed to know all about espionage from the book; 'Teach yourself how to be a Spy.' Jack wondered if BT ever led a normal life cooped up with a mad scientist for a dad.

'To set up your spy lock you pluck out one of your hairs and place it across the opening of your drawer. Then you get some Sellotape and fasten both ends of the hair in place making sure you smooth down the Sellotape with the back of your fingernail, that way, it becomes practically invisible,' BT had explained.

'And what is the point of all this?' Jack wanted to know at the time.

As Jack peered closely where he had set this 'hair trap' in place, he knew exactly what the point of the exercise was. His hair follicle had been rived out from one side of the Sellotape, the clearest indication that his drawer had been opened in his absence. With his dad at work and his mum seemingly vanished, then clearly someone else had been there.

The box had gone! He looked again with pajamas, socks and pairs of underpants flying in every direction, but still no wooden box. Although Jack knew which drawer he had hidden the box in, his brain told him to search all the drawers.

Still no luck! The only thing he succeeded in doing was turning his bedroom into a bombsite. Even if he could call the police, any evidence would have been wiped out by now.

What would the others think? Jack wanted to find the treasure more than anything in the world. It almost felt as though he had held the winning lottery ticket between his fingers, only for the wind to rip it out of his grasp. Jack's dream was blowing away into the distance. (22)

Chapter Twenty

E

"Have you told the cops?" asked BT slouching on a beanbag.

"What...yes, erm, I mean no," answered Jack.

"Well I think we should. This is way too deep for us, these creeps whoever they are, if they are prepared to break into your house in broad daylight, look like they mean business. Someone could get hurt." Jules feared.

"One reason is they wouldn't believe us and plus we'd have to tell them about the box and how we found it at that mansion. And then that Inspector Tyrrell is really creepy. We can't trust him. We have to do it. It's up to us," Jack spelled out.

"Yea but think about it logically," added Holly. "What would've happened if you had been at home? Do you think they would have knocked on your bedroom door and asked for it politely? And not only that, they've stolen the one clue that could lead us to the treasure."

"I hate to say this," Martin joined in. "I think Jack's right."

"Since when have you become Mr. serious?" asked Jules.

"But just think about it yeah. They know where Jack lives and they must know we're his friends.

They've probably got our every move covered. If it is that Inspector, then he'll have his cop buddies bugging our houses as we speak."

"Martin," Jack said. "I think you're making a very good case to say why we shouldn't be doing this."

"Am I?" Everyone burst out laughing.

"Come on, what do you say? We will never have another opportunity at a real adventure like this," Jack pleaded.

"Well actually I've been doing some research on the four corners and found out some fascinating stuff," Holly added.

"See, that's what I'm talking about. So what have you got for us then, Holly?"

"Well I searched everywhere on the net. And do you know what I found? Nothing!"

"And that's fascinating?" BT bleated.

"That's what I thought as well. So anyway I took the liberty of visiting Mr. Booth…"

"Who's he?" Jack whispered over to Jules.

"His history teacher."

"Oh right, thanks."

"Are you two listening?" Holly said impatiently. "Do you want to hear this or what? As I was saying, I knew he had a collection of antiquarian historical text books about medieval Europe. He'd always said I could go round anytime."

Holly explained, having looked through every ancient text, he found nothing. It was almost as if

The Four Corner's didn't exist. Just as he was about to give up, a manuscript slipped out from a tatty, dusty book. Within the passages the first word in every paragraph was penned differently. Those words were a code which made reference to the secret esoteric order.

Not only that but the three lions, so famous in history for Richard the First wasn't just a symbol of national pride and heritage. Holly discovered King Richard the Second used the three lion symbol for his secret plan.

Holly also discovered that King Richard the Second was part of The Four Corner's, but then created a splinter group, a quest to reunite the Lionheart. After his death, Richard the Lionhearts' body was buried in three separate locations. King Richard the Second wanted to bring together the three sections of the Lionhearts' buried body. A united Lionheart would bring unity to England once again and he had provided his vast wealth to realise that vision. A strong England would rule Europe. It was all about power.

"So are you saying that this is all about Richard the Lionheart's body?" asked BT.

"Yuck," Martin squeaked.

"Well sort of. But the second King Richard must have been quite high up in The Four Corner's and used his influence to get some from within to help him with his own personal quest," Holly explained.

"A bit like me asking BT to borrow his hover board because we're mates?" asked Jack.

"Well yeah, but you're missing the point. If you remember when Miss. White translated the note we found…"

"You mean I found," Jack corrected.

"What-ever!" Holly said. "As I was saying, the second Richard had bequeathed his own wealth for this reason. All these clues are what he had put in place to ensure that the gold didn't fall into the wrong hands."

"So Mr. Clever-clogs, if this King gave them his treasure, how come it's buried? Why didn't they take it and spend it on what they were asked to do?" Martin grinned.

"And," Jack added. "If he gave them that letter, how come it was hidden behind the stone?"

"I don't know. Maybe Admergill hid the note from the rest of the order and the treasure was never found. But I can tell you something for definite, King Richard the Second had not been buried in Kings Langley as many historians believe. This means we're not only on the trail of his hidden treasure, but on the verge of finding the truth about the kings final resting place as well," Holly beamed.

Jack couldn't believe that they were on the trail of mountains of gold, rubies and diamonds, yet all Holly was interested in was finding where the dead King was really buried. Momentarily everyone had forgotten they no longer possessed the next clue – the box had been stolen.

"And I never even got the chance to look at it," Jack gloomily pointed out. "We don't even know what was written on it."

"That's not entirely true," Jules said, stunning them into silence. "I think I know what's on the box."(9)

Chapter Twenty One

N

Fortune smiled upon them. Jules had taken some pictures of the box with her phone in the back of the car.

Minutes felt like hours as they waited for Jules to return with print outs of the pictures.

Jack stared intensely at a picture showing the top of the box. The crafted antique was varying shades of walnut from orangey-yellow to the darkest of browns. Squares containing two or three letters were inlaid into the wood in no apparent order. Smack bang in the centre was the letter 'X' on its own.

Jack was rubbish when it came to puzzles and passing the print to Martin, he moved onto the second picture. This picture was equally confusing with squiggly lines looking like strings of spaghetti and random images that didn't make any sense. He recognised one picture that looked like the cross of the four corners.

"What's that?" BT said, breaking Jack's concentration. "Look on the back of Jack's head, it's a tattoo!"

"Yea… it looks like a wheel or sommat," added Holly.

"Is ther'… where?" Martin joined in.

"It's not a tattoo, it's a birth mark. You can only

see it when I get my hair cut. Mum knows I hate my hair short."

"I thought it was a bit strange. If you're gonna have a tattoo, then you'd want something cool not a sissy wheel," Martin laughed. "Anyway I'm bored of guess the picture, who fancies going to Ghyll Church to see if any conkers are ready yet?"

"But what about the photos and the treasure?" Jack wanted to stay and solve the mystery.

He couldn't believe that they were on the verge of a huge discovery and all they were interested in was picking stupid conkers.

"Oh and Jack, my mum's been nagging me over my bike and I sort of need it back today, or she'll go bonkers at me," Martin explained. Not only did Jack have to sacrifice hunting his treasure, but he would have to miss out on the fun as well.

Jack wasn't sure if it was Thursday or Friday – that was the trouble during the summer holidays, days merged into weeks and weeks blurred into one another. One thing he did know is that the day was a scorcher. And it would be even hotter inside his grandad's living room.

Finally Jack turned into Dam Head Road and began slowly walking up the hill. He still didn't fully know his way around Barnoldswick, but the route to his grandad's was easy. He'd already taken his top off and tied it around his waist, but those final steps under the unforgiving, midday heat were almost unbearable.

No one used the front doors on this row of terraces, most likely because there was nowhere to drive a car. Jack like every other visitor opened the gate into the back yard. His grandads' yard was neat and compact. Martin's red bike leant against the powder blue park bench, exactly where he had left it.

Straight ahead was the front window to the living room. His grandad's strategic positioning of his chair meant he could just see above the gate, not missing anything. His whole life had come down to the comings and goings of a three foot wide section of Dam Head Road.

Jack looked to see him sat on his regal throne. Once given the nod of approval, he would be free to cross the threshold through the never-locked back door and into his domain. Something wasn't right.

There was a strange expression on his grandad's face and Jack was sure he gave a quick shake of the head. Jack froze when he realised someone else was there. A man walked in front of the window.

"What's up with you, old man?" Jack heard a muffled voice demand.

'Who does he think he's talking too?' Jack wanted to know. Charging through the house, he burst into the living room.

A short stocky man with shoulders wider than a football pitch hovered too close to Jack's grandad for his liking.

"Run Jack, run," his grandad called.

"What are you doing in here?" Jack demanded. "Now get out!" There was no way he was leaving his grandad.

"I'll call the police," he told the thug.

The man laughed before moving a couple of steps closer. Had Jack not made himself clear, what part of <u>get out</u> did the creep not understand? Before Jack could holler any louder, he caught a flash of metal in the man's hand. His eyes followed the hand movement hypnotically as the man brought it up towards his own face.

Jack snapped out of his trance. The thug had opened a switchblade knife to reveal its sharp blade. "You like this do you?" he asked, gently stroking the blade against the side of his leathery cheek. "You know what I want and I intend to have it. Otherwise things will turn ugly."

Jack shuffled backwards tripping over his own feet. Clambering back up he turned and ran through the door that led into the kitchen and sprinted towards help.

"Whoa there, fella. Where are you going in such a rush?"

Trapped tighter than a sardine in a tin! Jack tried kicking the stranger. The man's arms felt like rock as Jack was hauled back into the house. He was mercilessly dragged down some stone steps.

The man threw him onto the cold, stone floor before heading back up the stairs, locking the cellar door behind him.

Picking himself up, Jack looked around the insides of the cellar, objects filtered through the fog of his anger, as he built up a mental image of his surroundings. It was a small room with whitewashed walls in serious need of repainting. He couldn't see another way out, but he knew he must be missing something. Being in the basement under the house everywhere should have been dark, only there was light. He looked up to see a small window layered with grime.

Jack jumped onto a very old washing machine stood beneath the window. Rubbing a patch clean, he realised he was looking into his grandad's backyard, at ground level, the gate to freedom within his grasp.

It was then he spotted the latch.

His heart jumped into his mouth. The stupid ape had locked him in a room with an escape route.

Classic schoolboy error!

The latch however was tougher than he expected, solid with lack of use over the years. Finally he managed to lever it open. It was a tight squeeze even for his skinny frame, but in the end Jack managed to squirm through the small hole like a wriggly worm.

As quiet as a mouse Jack grabbed Martin's bike and slowly backed away from the house. If the man in the living room turned around now and looked out of the window, the game would be up.

Jack retreated slowly with one eye fixed on the house.

Only five steps to the gate... his heart was pounding.

Four steps to go.

Only three steps left... a torrent of sweat streamed down his forehead.

Two steps... his mind went blank.

Last step... his hand trembled as he fumbled for the gate latch. He could not take his eyes off the window.

'Please don't turn round,' Jack pleaded. Nearly there, just another second...

"Ouch!" Jack howled as Martin's bike clattered into the stone gate post. A combination of the bike and Jack crashing to the ground provided enough noise to wake a tree.

Jack looked helplessly towards the window in desperation. If only by some sheer miracle his captors had not heard.

Today his luck was out, the man turned around.

Chapter Twenty Two

B

St Mary's le-Ghyll was a very old church situated at the end of a country lane on the outskirts of Barnoldswick. A few horse chestnut trees—more affectionately known as 'conker trees'—lined the perimeter of the church grounds.

"Come on, Martin. It's useless chucking that stick up there. They're not ready yet," Holly stated the obvious.

"I know," answered Martin. "But, the tree's fuller than Mr. Grainer's class when he's giving away free chocolate. You'd think at least some would be ripe by now," Martin replied, crestfallen.

"Chocolate…who's given away free chocolate?" Holly wanted to know.

Jules and BT wandered through the church grounds waving sticks at the overgrown weeds. Because of the peaceful setting of the church, they would often come here. To the front of the church, as well as to its left, were mostly modern, well-cared-for gravestones.

They passed an area full of grand, ornate headstones standing proudly – if a gravestone could ever be said to be proud. These graves were much older, mainly dating back to the War. Some of the gravestones stood seven or eight feet tall.

The more interesting of the church features lay to its rear, an untamed jungle of wilderness adventure. BT and Jules fought their way through the tall, uncut grass. The gravestones in this area of the grounds had been overtaken by plants or eroded by time.

Finally the land fell away from the church rolling down to a small beck dotted with trees, perfect for messing around, away from prying eyes.

Jules stood staring at the eroded writing on one of the gravestones, she could just about make out the name Ruth Maycock. The two letters flashed before her eyes. She pulled out her phone to look at the pictures of the stolen box.

She had cracked the code.

***

Without a second thought, Jack jumped on Martin's bike and raced down the street. Tears streamed down his face, burning his cheeks. He did not understand what was happening. He narrowly missed a woman walking her dog. He heard words being shouted, but could not hear what was said.

No time to wait at the zebra crossing, he bunny hopped the kerb and hurtled across the road. The thought of gold and jewels was no longer important. His dreams paled into insignificance compared with the safety of his grandad.

Blindly, Jack rode on when, the noise of an engine

revving hard cut through the sound of his heart booming against his rib cage. He glanced over his shoulder in time to see a white van gaining on him – fast!

Jack had no chance of outrunning them. The van was practically upon him and if it touched his wheel, it would all be over. He saw a turning on his left just a few yards away.

The van was too fast and he would never make it. In a flash Jack mounted the kerb. A street lamp prevented the van from following him onto the pavement.

Breathlessly, Jack leaned the bike hard to his left and turned into a short street. Thankfully, it was downhill, but he had no time to rest. He could hear the roar of the engine from the white van as it entered the street. The short row of terrace houses soon came to an end. If he could keep his pursuers on these narrow streets, he might just have a chance, he hoped.

The street ended and, Jack swung the bike to his right. He could hear the sound of crunching gears before the screech of tyres as rubber burned a trail on the tarmac.

Jack hastily peddled along the narrow road between the backs of two rows of terraces. Ahead, a parked car blocked the road. His bike would easily slip through the gap whereas the van had no chance. It was just a question of whether he would make it in time. The parked car wasn't far now, but his energy levels were fading fast.

The van was closing in. Jack glanced over his shoulder as the van crashed through a line of washing strung across the narrow back-street.

A deafening screech as the van hit the brakes told him they wouldn't make it. Jack cycled past the parked car, buying a few precious seconds. He reached the top of the street at the same time as the van reversed the short distance to the bottom.

The clock was ticking. "Think Jack, think!" he muttered trying to catch his breath now he was back at the main road.

"The canal!"

If he could make it to the canal towpath, they wouldn't be able to follow him. But it was too far and he would never reach it in time.

He spotted a 4X4 driving along the main road a few hundred yards away. Within seconds, the pickup was almost in line with him.

He only had one shot at grabbing its tailgate and hitching a ride. He kicked down firmly on the pedals. Jack reached out, his arm clutching at thin air as the pickup went sailing past. His heart sank.

The horn of the 4X4 blasted as it skidded to a halt. Some kids playing football had kicked their ball onto the main road, causing the pickup to stop.

With one Herculean effort Jack reached the truck just before it pulled away. Unbeknown to the driver, the vehicle now had two extra wheels to power.

Finally Jack was able to catch his breath. He then heard the one noise he was dreading, the screech of a vehicle joining the main road at high speed.

The guy in the Mitsubishi Animal was no slowcoach. They were in a thirty zone and he must have been doing at least forty-five. There was only one slight problem with this – the bad guys were going faster.

Jack's lift began to climb the hill. The canal was at the top. He was nearly there but realised he was on the wrong side of the truck. He needed to move across the back and into the outside lane. The van was accelerating fast behind him.

A car was travelling in the opposite direction. The opening to the canal path was there, but on the other side of the road. The white van was almost on him while the approaching car blocked his escape route.

Jack had no choice. He had to take the risk!

Clenching his eyes shut Jack let go of the truck. The loud beeping of a car horn sounded, ringing through every inch of his head. Every second he could hear it meant another second he was still alive.

Bang!

Opening his eyes, he realised he was still in one piece. The bike's front wheel had hit the kerb. The damaged wheel wobbled uncontrollably as he rode and bumped his way down the steps that led to the safety of the canal.

CHAPTER TWENTY TWO

The canal wasn't wide enough for a motor vehicle to travel along, but just to be one hundred percent sure they had not followed him, Jack took one last look over his shoulder. (15)

Chapter Twenty Three

E

It wouldn't be safe to go home, they knew where Jack lived. He needed to think. A voice inside his head told him to try the summerhouse.

Pushing his way through the conifer hedge at the bottom of the Brown's garden felt like stepping through the doorway to another world – their secret world. Along the narrow passage, he walked with a sense of urgency and passed through the gate that led into Simon King's garden.

Jack could hear the sound of a small motorised engine as he ran towards the summerhouse.

It was deserted!

He remembered something about a church but couldn't concentrate, the noise was getting louder. Distracted from his mission, he turned to see a motorised lawnmower travelling towards him with Simon behind the wheel.

"Hello James," Holly's uncle shouted over the roar of the engine.

"It's Jack," he hollered.

"What's that," Simon replied now inches from where he stood.

Jack could not be bothered correcting him. Forgetfulness seemed to be a grownup thing.

Finally Simon cut the engine. "What are you up

too?"

"I'm looking for the others and was hoping they might be here."

"Oh I see. Well as you can see they are not. But if you want to wait for them, you are most welcome."

"I'd better not. I'm in a sort of rush."

"Are you sure? You can come up to the house and have some refreshments. I can try giving them a ring. I think I've got Shaun's number somewhere."

Everything Simon said made sense. Jack could spend all evening running around trying to find them. If only his parents would buy him a mobile phone.

"Just wait here while I go and have a look for his number. I think I've got it somewhere in my office," Simon explained as they entered the house.

This was the second time Jack had been in Simon's house. He remembered the conversation he had overheard between Simon and Danny from the antiques shop the last time he was here.

Jack was sure Danny had sold a coin to Simon by mistake and Danny now wanted it back, the easy way or the hard way.

Danny must be responsible for sending those heavies round to his grandad's and it would only be a matter of time before they showed up here. Whatever Simon had inadvertently bought from him, it was obvious Danny would stop at nothing.

"Here we go then..." Simon said stopping

midsentence.

Without waiting for Simon to give him Holly's phone number, Jack ran through the Brown's garden and out onto St Mary's Avenue. Nowhere felt safe anymore. On his way to the church he ran past BT's house and could have sworn he spotted him through the living room window.

Jack rushed down the steps and slammed the elephant door knocker onto the brass plate, creating a sonic boom. Waiting those few seconds seemed an eternity. Just when he had the sinking feeling nobody was home, the door swung wide open. He was greeted by an exact replica of BT, only much older. Strapped to his head was a pair of weird looking goggles with a single antenna.

You would have thought Jack was not even there the way the man peered beyond him, with a quick look right and then left. He appeared nuttier than a squirrel.

Without saying a word, Jack was hauled through the door and it slammed shut behind him. Before Jack could protest he heard a familiar voice.

"Jack." It was Jules. "I'm so glad to see you. The box, the box…" she kept repeating.

Jack wanted to ask who had manhandled him through the door, but with all the bad guys, his grandad in danger, possibly his parents too, and Jules now talking about the box, his head was like scrambled eggs.

"Finally! Where have you been?" Martin quipped, appearing with Holly. The whole gang was reunited in BT's kitchen.

"Martin, shut it will you?" Jules berated her brother.

Martin looked back with a blank 'What have I done?' expression.

"What box?" Jack asked.

"You know the box you found at Towneley hall?"

"What? The one that was stolen…"

"You remember I took some photos of it. Well, it's not a box at all. It's a map!" Jules beamed triumphantly.

"Oh great," Jack replied with a lack of enthusiasm.

"What's with the fish face?" Martin jeered.

"Yeah, why aren't you excited?" Jules asked.

Jack was excited. This was all he ever cared about, or so he thought. With the situation changing, he realised other things were more important.

"What's up?" Jules asked, surprised.

"They're holding my grandad hostage," Jack blurted out. "They got me too, but I managed to escape. And now I don't know what to do." He could feel his voice begin to crack.

An eerie silence fell upon the kitchen.

"But you always know what to do. That's why I followed you into this treasure hunt," Holly was the first to speak.

"Well, I think we should tell the police," BT

remonstrated.

"No," Jules emphatic reply shocked the others. "That police Inspector is in on this, I bet you. We can't trust them…"

"Come on, Jack," Jules begged. "This is our chance. We can find the gold. Then we can go to the government, or something. We can't let them win. And besides, what if they want to get rid of the evidence? Have you ever thought of that?"

"What do you mean?" Jack asked, puzzled.

"We know too much," Jules continued. "Think about it, Jack! If they are as ruthless as you say they are, do you think they are going to let us run around blabbing about it to everyone?"

Jack stood in silence while his brain began to compute all the variables. As if in slow motion, his brain processed each option, unfurling the results of his thought process and reading the decision. Half of him wanted to end it right now while the other half wanted to find the gold, call the police, and kick the bad guys' butts.

This is your only chance, began indelibly writing on the back of his corneas in thick, black, permanent marker.

"Okay," Jack sighed. "But we have to be quick, so we can find the treasure and then call the cops, before they realise anything is up. So what have we got?"

"I'd thought you'd never ask," Holly piped up.

"Ghyll Church or St Mary-le-Ghyll to be precise was apparently built in 1157..."

"So it's definitely well old," Martin interrupted.

"Interestingly, extra work was carried out in the fourteenth century." Holly hung on his last few words.

Holly was writing on the kitchen table! As Jack looked closer he could see he was actually writing on a large sheet of paper fastened with Sellotape and stuck to the table.

"King Richard the Second, Admergill, and the Barons' Clifford and Towneley all lived during the same time period of the fourteenth century." With each name, Holly began writing on the paper in a green marker. "Sorry about the colour of the ink, unfortunately it was all BT had..."

"Yeah, well, I'm providing everything else, aren't I?"

"I wasn't complaining, was I?" Holly defended.

"Okay, Okay. We will never get anywhere unless you two <u>shut up</u>!" Jules chided them.

"Yeah, sorry about that. Anyway, as I was saying, we also know about this secret esoteric order..."

"What's 'esoteric' mean?" Jack whispered to Martin to avoid interrupting Holly's precious history lesson.

"I think 'historic' means 'old'," Martin replied. "But I'm not too sure, I lost track of what he was saying ages ago. I've haven't a clue what he's on-about."

"Yeah, me too," Jack yawned. "Anyway we'd better be quiet or he'll go cyclone on us if he thinks we aren't listening."

"…where there doesn't seem to be any historical records mentioning their existence. Which means this wasn't just some silly secret club, but this was major top secret business." Holly paused for emphasis, he was in his element.

"We know they were known as the four corners. And, we also know that King Richard the Second set up a splinter group to reunite the various parts of Richard the Lionhearts' body and bring them back to England and this was symbolised by the three lions. So King Richard arranged… What have you got your hand up for, Martin? This isn't class."

"I know. But I've got a question. Which Richard are you on about now?"

"King Richard the Second," Holly huffed at Martin's stupidity. It was clearly obvious who he had been talking about.

"Can we not have code names, like Ricky and Rocky? That way we would know…"

"Don't be such a royal mongo. Now, if you don't stop interrupting, then we will never get out of BT's kitchen…

King Richard the Second commissioned his fellow order members to use his wealth because he knew he was dying. And my guess is that these said same individuals had already placed the clues in their building projects as markers to the whereabouts of the wealth. But the question is; if your grandad really did stumble across the King's fortune Jack, why hadn't they used it?" Holly continued.

A discussion broke out about who had hidden the letter and key behind the brick and why. The more they talked about it, the more confused Jack became. He tried to work out how the King's friend had stored it behind the brick for safe keeping, but Jules soon extinguished his theory.

Everything seemed back to front, the coin which was part of the treasure led to the note and the note led to the treasure, they were missing a vital piece of the jigsaw. But unless a man who had been dead for over six hundred years came back and told them why, they may never find out.

Thankfully, Jules moved the conversation back to the present day. "Listen a minute. While we were messing around up at Ghyll Church looking for conkers, me and BT wandered down to the long, scruffy grass. It was here that I saw one of the old gravestones peeking out. I could just about read the name Ruth Maycock... Shurrup Martin – he always laughs at that name – so immature!" Jules digressed.

"Well what is so important about that name?" Jack asked, getting Jules back on track.

"On its own? Nothing," replied Jules, patiently. "But, when I stumbled over another gravestone with the name: James Harvey Smith, that's when it clicked."

"Who's he? I've never heard of him," remarked Jack. He was getting impatient with Jules' prolonged tale.

"No one ... 'The who' ... That's not important," answered Jules. Taking a deep breath, she resumed her tale. "Something hit me about the photos of the box."

Jack stood and watched as her lips opened and closed. She wasn't making any sense at all.

"...Jack, are you even listening?"

"Er, yeah," he replied somewhat distractedly. Just then, a little numbskull character wandered into a dark corner of Jack's brain and pulled a cord. A light bulb pinged on. Excitedly, Jack encouraged Jules to finish her summary. He guessed what she was going to say next. (18)

Chapter Twenty Four

N

"The letters on the box we found in the photo I took…" Jules continued patiently. "In the top left hand corner, one of the squares contains the letters RM. Then across the box on the right, but lower down are the letters JHS. And not only are they the same as the people's names on the gravestones but they are in the exact same locations as the tombstones in the graveyard. This isn't a box where the secrets are hidden on the inside; they're here in plain view on the outside. It's a map!" she finished triumphantly.

"It's more brilliant than getting a birthday cake when it's not even your birthday," Martin remarked about their find.

While all this had been going on BT had been busy kitting out two rucksacks with hi-tech equipment. BT announced they were now packed with everything they needed for the treasure hunt, which was, in fact, a <u>real</u> treasure hunt. He then handed out a watch to everyone with instructions to synchronise!

Knock! Knock!

***

Inspector David Tyrrell stood outside the dark green front door and knocked. This was his town and he was determined to get answers.

No reply. Not to worry, the Inspector knew Jack had friends. He now walked towards the faded red door with a spring in his step.

He knocked again, peering through the frosted glass into the kitchen; he could make out the silhouette of a person.

It was too nice a day for running around on a fool's errand. A shadowy shape shifted from side to side behind the glass panel. At last he had found someone in, his time wasn't wasted. Finally a key turned in the lock.

A middle aged woman stood there with a towel wrapped about her head. She looked surprised.

"Can I help you? I'm rather busy," she snapped.

"Is your mother in?" he smiled.

"I'm the mother," she cooed.

"I am terribly sorry, how silly of me. Allow me to introduce myself. I'm the Inspector from the local constabulary. We are just trying to locate your son and Jack Hunter. Don't worry, it's nothing to be alarmed about, they're helping us with a small matter." The Inspector knew there was no need to cause alarm.

"I'm afraid he's not here, none of them are. Perhaps you should try the Bakers, next door... that-a-way," Mrs. Hollingsworth said as she stepped out from the doorway, enough to be able to point him in the right direction.

"Are you sure my Shaun's not in any trouble?"

"Quite sure," he smiled, already stepping out through the gate.

Inspector Tyrrell walked down the last few steps before negotiating his way around a rusting lawn mower that barred his path. Finally he walked the short distance to the front door of number sixty four, the Baker residence. A brass knocker in the shape of an elephants head was fixed to the dark wooden door.

Bang! Bang!

The elephants head struck the brass plate. Inspector Tyrrell let the knocker drop from his grasp and began to wring his hands in eager anticipation.

*****

BT dropped their backpacks onto the kitchen table before leaving the kitchen to answer the front door. The others waited. Jack thought it sounded like someone was attempting to smash through the front door rather than just knocking.

"Skull and cross bones," Martin blurted out for no apparent reason.

"That's pirates, you muppet," his sister berated him.

"I do know! But I always wanted to find skull and

crossbones. It makes the thought of buried treasure more real," Martin explained.

"BT's been gone a long time, don't you think?" Holly pointed out, looking worried.

The kitchen door began to slowly edge open. All eyes were riveted to the door. BT emerged. He explained it was only the milkman wanting payment and he had to run upstairs to get it from his mum, who was in bed with a migraine.

Martin suggested throwing jam bombs at the baddies. Then, when they were being chased, they could lead them to a wasp's nest. The wasps would know what to do then. Jules quickly pointed out that they didn't know the location at this moment in time of any wasp's nest, or even a beehive for that matter. Martin decided to leave the ideas alone, much to Jack and everybody else's relief.

"Make sure I've got the bag with the chocolate in," said Holly.

"Is that all you're bothered about?" said BT.

"Food is the fuel for cortex consumption..." Holly responded defensively.

Jack and Holly each grabbed a rucksack and a walkie-talkie. Holly volunteered to carry a rucksack, if only to make sure he would not be separated from the munchies.

***

A woman's head appeared in the upstairs window. "Can I help?" she called down.

From what Inspector Tyrrell could make out, the woman was still in her nightdress. This was a bit surprising as the afternoon had nearly passed by. But, again, he learned that he had missed them.

"But," she added just as he was pulling his mobile phone out of his pocket and proceeding to plan 'B', "I believe Anthony mentioned something about Ghyll Church."

Inspector Tyrrell was back on the trail!

"If you go to the top of the street and turn right up Ben Lane, you'll see a footpath to your left. There's a small wooden style into the field. Just follow the footpath over the hill and it will take you straight there. It's just about a mile," she told him.

He knew how to get there and he definitely would not be walking. It was only a matter of time.

Chapter Twenty Five

E

The gravestones looked old with many dating as far back as the War. Although this was ancient to Jack, what they were seeking needed to be five hundred years older.

They continued through the graveyard towards the rear of the church.

"How come the other graves are well tended but this area has been left alone?" Jack asked with no reply.

It all seemed unreal. Any minute he half expected to spot a camera peering at them from behind a tree, or someone dressed in a fake skeleton outfit to jump in front of them for some television hoax game show.

They fought their way through the abnormally long grass until Jules, photo of the map in hand, halted.

"Right then, RM was up there," she pointed to her left, "and here is JHS which means the grave marked with an X should be round about...here."

There was no sign of a gravestone where Jules indicated, just a wizened, ivy-covered tree.

"Perhaps the stone's fallen down," suggested Martin.

"Or it doesn't exist," lamented Jack who was

beginning to think this was just another wild goose chase. Still, curiosity pulled him towards the strange tree like ferrous filings unavoidably drawn to a magnet.

"Ouch," Jack yelped as he tripped over something hidden by the long grass.

Jack wanted to inflict serious pain on whatever had hurt him. His hand struck something hard and cold. He wanted to hurl it as far as he could throw it. To his surprise, he discovered a low wall – hidden in the undergrowth.

Ten minutes later, Jack stood back to admire his find. They had found the grave marked 'X' hidden underneath Mother Nature. The shrivelled tree was actually growing out of the middle of the grave. A combination of the tree and creepers covering the headstone had obscured it from sight. The whole plot was the size of his mum and dad's Ford Fiesta with the headstone standing vertically, out of the ground.

In the centre of the gravestone was the cross of the four corners. The mark indicated by the 'X' on the picture symbolised the cross. King Richard the Second had left a mark to indicate where he or his treasure had been buried.

Jack slung the rucksack off his back and pulled out two pieces of paper. One was the parchment he had found with the key and the other was a sheet of standard A4, plain paper. With Miss. White's initial help, Holly and Jules doing their own research, they had fully translated the letter carrying the dying king's last requests. Jack unfolded the two pieces of paper.

Jules relayed the words on the gravestone.

'The secret to life is at the centre of death.
Remember me as you   pass by
As you are now, so once was I
As I am now so you must be
Therefore, prepare to follow
*   me.'*

"I don't get it? Is this some sort of a clue? Or even a riddle?" asked Jack.

"Hang on a minute," Jules answered, repeating the phrase under her breath. "It doesn't mean anything. It's just a poem – a bit like the message written inside a sympathy card."

The others looked at her blankly.

"It's basically saying we all die. Just as the king did, then so will we. We have to be prepared to follow him, meaning he went to the grave and so will we," she said.

"It's a bit grim, don't you think? Who'd want to put something so morbid in a symphony card?" Martin asked.

"Not symphony..." Jules began. "Oh, never mind," she sighed.

Jack was not listening. He was too busy looking at

the writing on the parchment and then the headstone. "That's odd, though don't you think?" he noted. "In the original letter, the five lines of text are normal. But, on the stone, these two words 'pass by' are separate, further to one side of the tombstone. Then the word 'me' is written under 'follow'," he said, pointing to the stone as he spoke.

"Perhaps the person carving the stone wasn't being paid enough," joked BT. He then realised Martin had vanished and so had Holly.

"Holly? ... MARTIN, HOLLY?" BT yelled.

In the distance, they heard a mumbled reply. "Did that just sound like Holly with a mouth full of food to you? Does he ever stop?" Jack laughed.

"NO," Jules and BT both replied in unison. "Martin must have gone to get him."

"Wait up. You said 'me' was written under 'follow'. This might be a clue after all," Jules stared intently at the gravestone. "So, in other words, if we wanted to follow him, we would have to go under. I think it's telling us to go down into it."

"Jules that's brilliant..." exclaimed BT.

"What, you mean we have to go into the grave? Not on your life," Jack shuddered.

"If we look at it all again... 'Pass by' has been moved over to the right? So if I was to pass by to the right of the stone, right...let's see. BT, have you got anything I might be able to use for leverage in there?"

"I can do better than that," BT replied pulling a crowbar from the rucksack Jack had dumped on the ground.

"Who on earth carries a crowbar around with them?" Jack asked in disbelief.

A couple of minutes passed with all three of them trying to jemmy, push and heave the headstone open. It refused to budge. Hundreds of years stuck in the same position had literally cemented it in place.

Jack slumped to the ground while Jules, not wanting to give up, looked at the note again. He wanted a drink, but all the cans of pop, plus the chocolate and crisps were in the backpack Holly carried.

Jules' face lit up, like the moment, you spot a twenty-pound note lying on the pavement.

"Look at this!" she exclaimed, moving to the front of the grave again. "The message on the parchment doesn't have the fancy cross in the middle of the writing. But, it's been carved onto the centre of the gravestone."

She leaned forward and brushed her hand over the stone clearing away the lichens. "The secret of life is at the centre of death. This has to be it! The secret of life is...knowledge. Yes! Knowledge of knowing you are going to die one day. The centre of death is this cross, or 'X' marks the spot..." she finished triumphantly.

Jules pressed her thumb down in the centre of the

cross. They held their breath and waited with anticipation.

The diamond shape in the centre of the cross disappeared backwards into the stone. Jules was now able to put her finger into the hole and pull the rest of the cross outwards, in the same motion as you would a doorknocker – or even a lever. A loud clunk resounded from the ground under their feet.

Jules now marched smugly around the tree again to the right hand side of the large upstanding stone.

"As you pass by," she said with a big cheesy grin. Then with both hands placed on the side of the header stone, she pushed. With minimum effort, the massive piece of stone started to slide in the direction she pushed until it must have hit an internal bumper and stopped with a thud.

"Pass me a torch?" she asked casually. "...Therefore prepare to follow under me." Jules shone a beam of light into a dark hole that had opened up in the ground. "Yep, there are steps leading down," she announced before spinning around to face them. "Well, are you coming or what?" she demanded, glaring impatiently at the others.

At that, she began to disappear into the ground. (22)

Chapter Twenty Six

A

Martin's plan was to sneak up behind Holly and make him jump. Playing tricks on people was his favourite pastime. As he was searching for Holly, he saw three unsavoury looking men marching towards the church. That is when he recognised the man in front.

Martin spotted Holly standing at the side of a stone out-building. The thugs were heading straight towards him. Martin would be too late to help.

The others! He had to warn them.

***

Holly dumped his backpack on the ground. He needed brain food. A chocolate fix was in order, he convinced himself, tucking into a Mars bar. He was half way through his snack when he heard BT shout his and Martin's names. "Okay," he replied with his mouth half full, "I'm coming!"

"Red sky at night; shepherd's pie for tea," muttered Holly, craving the thought of a delicious, piping hot, shepherd's pie, with chips and gravy of course.

Holly fiddled with the watch BT had given them, again. He still could not believe BT had gotten his hands on something so hi-tech. He pressed the green button once more and watched a luminous green digital image shine out from the centre of the dial, hovering millimetres above the watch face.

BT had explained it was just a map with a GPS tracking device built in. Holly stared at the five dots moving on the ghostly image. His dot was red while the other four were blue. He could see three of the dots were quite away from his, but one lone blue dot flickered close by. 'Martin,' he laughed to himself.

He was about to pick up his rucksack when he heard footsteps crunching on the gravel path. Holly was not about to let brainless Martin catch him out and he crouched behind the stone outhouse.

He was poised, ready to jump out at Martin.

"Gotcha," Holly shouted, colliding with a large, bulky figure. "I'm sorry, mister…" he started to say.

A large man in white overalls towered above him, a tattoo on the side of his beefy neck poked out from under his collar.

Holly's brain told him to run but his legs would not react.

The man grabbed hold of him. Holly could feel the powerful vice-like grip around his waist. He wrestled helplessly.

"So where are they then?" another man calmly asked.

Holly received a shock when he turned round. There standing in from of him was a man with a shaven head, dressed in a scruffy tee shirt and jogging bottoms.

It was Danny Pullen.

"Where are who?" Holly replied as cool as an ice cube.

"Don't play games with me."

The man holding Holly began to crush him. "Over there," Holly wheezed, nodding towards the church.

"You see! You do have your uses." He turned to the man holding Holly and ordered. "Now tie him up."

"What... I did what you asked," protested Holly, kicking out at the tattooed thug. "Gerroff me!" he screeched.

"You can't bind genius you know." Holly shouted, wriggling in vain.

"Okay, if that's how you want to play it…" replied the man holding him. Holly's world blacked out. (8)

Chapter Twenty Seven

T

Jules disappeared into the ground. BT handed Jack an odd-looking piece of equipment which he could only describe as a torch, with straps.

Desperate to know if Martin and Holly were safe Jack looked up in time to see Martin charging through the undergrowth.

"They're here..." Martin gasped between breaths.

"Who's here? Where's Holly?" said Jack.

That was when Jack suddenly saw the terror etched across Martin's face. He had never seen such an expression–until earlier today. Martin had the same terrified look his grandad had worn.

"The bad guys!" Martin blurted out. "And they've captured Holly."

This meant Jack's only option was to enter the tomb. He froze on the edge of the steps.

"There is no way I'm going into a grave," Jack protested. "There might be vampires or mummies." The very thought sent an icy chill through his body.

As quick as a flash, Martin ran past him and into the black abyss.

Jack was standing alone outside the tomb. When he looked around the church grounds, it looked a lot creepier than he recalled five minutes ago, the daylight already melting away.

Jack hesitated before stepping into the grave. He then had a flash of brilliance and grabbed a broken tree branch lying close by, covered in ivy and gnarled with age. He pulled the branch over the hole to cover their tracks as he entered the tomb.

Jack fumbled for the switch of his head torch, which he now had strapped securely around his head. A powerful beam of light shone out from the centre of his forehead.

A cold chill washed over him as he stepped off the bottom stone step. An hour ago, he never would have dreamed about standing inside a grave.

Jack spun around in every direction, looking for anything that remotely resembled treasure. They were inside an underground chamber and yet the ceiling was high enough to stand in. The tomb was roughly the same size of his grandad's living room, except this place had cobwebs covering the walls and was full of bones.

Using the bright torch Jack scoured the walls. It appeared to be a dead end, no door, no other way out.

Just then, a noise interrupted his thoughts. It sounded like bone smashing against solid stone. The sound echoed around the chamber.

"What are you doing?" Jack demanded.

"I don't really know, the skull looked like a football and I just kicked it," replied Martin after volleying a human skull against the inside of the tomb's wall.

"Are you mad? These bones are sacred. You'll end up bringing a voodoo curse down on us or sommat."

"Look on the wall over here." BT interrupted them. "Some sort of picture."

They rushed over to BT. On the wall was a painting of a small boat. It depicted a man heading towards an embankment, using a tall stick to push the boat. A person appeared to be offering his hand out.

"None of this makes any sense." Jack lamented. "It's just another rotten, dead end."

"And now we're trapped. Those thugs will be here any minute and they'll get us too," Martin added, still upset.

"There must be something on the photo," Jules said, shining the light on the others. "You wouldn't have gone to the trouble of putting the map on the box and then..."

They all stood and stared at where Jules reckoned the door should be according to the map.

"It's got to be here somewhere." Just a blank wall covered in cobwebs and tree roots. "This can't be a dead end," Jules complained, deep in concentration.

"And all we've found is some pathetic, old picture of a man in a boat," said Jack.

"Here let me look at that painting again," insisted Jules.

Jack figured they were wasting precious time and

suggested checking the map on the photograph again. Jules ignored him.

"Of course," she said. "Look! The picture is the same as on the box. I should have realised it sooner. I'm sure it's Charon."

"Who's Sharon?" asked Jack. He wished he knew all the stuff that Jules did. If only he had paid more attention in class. Again, he vowed he would change his classroom ways when school started again.

"Not Sharon... Charon! He was the ferryman in Greek mythology who ferried the dead to the underworld."

"Well what's that got to do with being in a grave?" asked Jack, bewildered.

"Nothing, unless it's supposed to indicate..." Jules stopped. "Jack have you got that coin with you?" she asked. "The one your grandad gave you." Jack pulled it from his pocket and begrudgingly passed it to Jules.

"How simple and yet so clever," Jules pointed out.

"What is? I don't get it," Martin moaned, his voice echoing inside the tomb.

"If anyone broke in here, well, they would be after only one thing, the treasure. Thieves only want to take, not give. Don't you see?" Jules said. "Look there at that small slot next to the picture of the ferryman."

"But that's just some crack in the stone," Jack protested.

"Well that's where you'd be wrong! On the picture, it shows someone paying the ferryman and unless I'm a monkey's uncle... I bet you put this coin in here..."she demonstrated.

"Don't do that," Jack shouted, rushing to stop her. "My grandad gave me that."

Too late!

Jules dropped the coin through the slot in the wall. All Jack could do was watch as it disappeared out of sight.

A red mist descended upon Jack. That coin belonged to his grandad!

The heavy sound of stone rumbling caused Jack to turn in time to see a section of wall slide open.

They had discovered the door. (18)

Chapter Twenty Eight

H

As they stepped through the opened doorway, Jack was convinced they would be walking into a cave full of treasure. To his dismay, they had entered an empty, rectangular room, with another door on the far wall.

He heard a clattering sound like a tin can rolling down a cobbled hill. A small object flew out of the wall. For a second, Jack thought it was just another trick.

The object glinted in the light from his torch, his grandad's gold coin! The ferryman with the girl's name had given it back to him. As Jack rushed to retrieve his coin, he heard Martin shout from behind, "Jack, you idiot, you forgot your backpack."

The coin landed in the middle of the floor, and spun on its edge before falling over.

"Jack... NO!" Jules shouted.

As Jack bent down to pick it up, he felt a section of the floor tilt forwards. A noise his brain could only describe as stone grinding against stone made him jump. The door that was supposed to be their exit was closing.

"Martin, the door!" Jack heard BT scream.

Jack turned in time to see the door they entered through also shutting. Martin was stuck in the first chamber, where they had paid the ferryman.

"Quick, grab something to jam it with," Jules ordered.

Jack hesitated for a second, not knowing which way to run, before turning and running towards the exit, only to get there as it slammed shut. He banged his clenched hands against the stone – but not too hard, it hurt. At the same time, he heard a crunching sound that echoed in the underground cavern.

"You stupid idiot," he heard Jules shout. "A bone... a bone? What use is a bone? Why didn't you use one of those big stones?" she wailed.

The door that Martin was stuck behind was partially open. The piece of bone stopped the door from fully closing, but with only enough room for a rat to squeeze through.

"It's not my fault," Jack heard Martin reply, from the other side of the door. "I didn't leave the backpack behind."

It was true. Martin was stuck, trapped on the other side of a solid two-foot, stone door, because of Jack. The bad guys could be here at any second, meaning Martin would have about as much chance as a fish in a small pond being hunted by a fisherman with a stick of dynamite.

"Go and get help," advised Jules.

"B-but," stammered Martin.

"Go, get out, now!" she ordered.

Chunks of rubble started to fall from the ceiling as

the walls began to shake.

"The floor," BT yelled.

Jack looked down. He was now standing on a narrow ledge about six inches wide. The floor was slowly moving away from him. Jack was trapped at the opposite end of the room to Jules and BT.

He looked down only to wish he hadn't. You should never look down!

A black hole was emerging. As he lit up the dark, big void, he saw large spears sticking up out of the ground.

Seconds ago, Martin was in the frying pan. Now, Jack, Jules and BT were one-hundred-percent in the fire and it was getting hotter. He wished he could think of a way out, a plan, anything at all. Very soon Jules and BT would have nowhere left to stand.

"Jack, look, over there," he heard Jules shout above the drone of the retracting floor. "There's some handles."

Handles or no handles, if Jules was pointing where he thought she was pointing, she had better think again. He did not intend to shuffle along the narrow ledge, all that way!

"Jack, it's our only chance," he heard her scream, again. Only this time he detected a tremble in her voice.

If only, there was some other way.

He placed his right foot gingerly to his side, clutching at the wall for security. The handles must be the width of a swimming pool away. Slowly he edged along. He was there sooner than he imagined and carefully turned to face the wall.

In front of him were four stone handles, evenly spaced, with four different images carved into the stone around each one.

"What am I supposed to do?" he yelled.

"What can you see?" Jules replied.

"Four stone handles sticking out with different pictures around each of them," he reported.

"I think you're supposed to turn each handle towards a picture, like a combination to a lock!" Jules explained.

"Well, which should I turn first?" Jack shouted.

"I don't know," she replied.

Jack looked at the first handle and muttered, "Eeny-meeny-miny-mo," closed his eyes and turned the furthest handle from him towards its first picture.

Nothing happened.

Then the ground began to tremble underfoot. The floor he was standing on slowly retracted by three more inches. He nearly lost his balance and only managed to stay on the ledge by standing on his tiptoes.

"Did anything happen?" Jules shouted.

"Did anything happen ... are you kidding me? I nearly ended up as sushi. That's what happened!" Jack responded hysterically.

"Well, if you don't hurry up, we'll be joining you,"

BT hollered.

"What does the map say? The clues gotta be on there," Jack pleaded.

"There is nothing except a picture of the cross of The Four Corners," Jules shouted.

"The four corners, of course!"

Jules flashed her light up towards the roof, to the corner of the room where Jack was clawing on for grim life. "It's the corners," she shouted back. "Does that first handle you turned have a picture of an elephant?"

Jack was not in the mood for games, but he was clean out of options. He looked at the furthest handle and the four pictures surrounding it. The second picture definitely looked like an elephant.

"Yeah," he replied, gasping for air while his calf muscles felt like they were on fire.

"Well, turn it, then."

Not needing a second invitation, he strained for the handle, turning it towards the elephant. The floor underneath began to shake underfoot, again. His strength failed as his hand began to slip.

The floor moved outwards, giving him back the stolen three inches. At last, he could stand properly again. His muscles ached, bulging in places he did not know existed.

"The second one is an arrow," she instructed. "And please...hurry up." Jules sounded desperate. The floor where they stood was nearly gone. Any second, both Jules and BT would fall.

To his relief, there was a picture of an arrow. He was just about to turn the handle towards it when he realised all the four pictures were arrows, facing in opposite directions.

"Which way is the arrow pointing?" he demanded.

"Er sideways," she trembled.

They were two arrows pointing sideways. "But which way is it pointing?"

"LEFT!" she shrieked in a pitch so high, the echo nearly made his ears bleed. He turned it as fast as he could.

To Jules and BT's relief the floor beneath them stopped moving with inches to spare.

"That was too close," said a relieved Jules. "Right, for the next one look for a pyramid."

There was a pyramid and after Jack turned the handle towards it, the floor began rumbling again, only this time it was closing. Finally, after he had turned the fourth handle, the door opened.

"The mark of the four corners on the map was the clue. Only this time it was literal. In each corner of this room near the ceiling was carved a picture and each picture was the key to the puzzle. Very clever!" Jules said, as they waited for the last few feet of the floor to snap shut.

All three stepped through the doorway, glad to be out of the room.

As they stepped through the opened doorway,

instead of walking into a cave full of treasure, they were standing in a dark, cold, horrible smelling passageway.

"My night-vision sensors are detecting something ahead," said BT.

"What, you've got night-vision goggles? That's so cool," Jack was amazed.

"I don't know what it is," continued BT looking worried. "But it's big... and it's heading this way, fast!" he exclaimed.

At first, they could hear the hum of a small engine that sounded like Simon's motorised lawnmower. It was rapidly getting louder. Soon it sounded more like a herd of wailing banshees. Jack did not know if wailing banshees travelled in herds, but under the present circumstances, he did not care.

"Bats! Get down," BT screamed.

Without arguing, Jack threw himself onto the hard, damp ground and placed his hands over his head.

"Urgh!" he screamed. "Could this get any worse?" he wanted to shout out as a multitude of screeching winged beasts raced overhead.

Jack felt his skin crawl at the very thought of them. Then he realised his skin was crawling, literally. Something was creeping across his neck.

Jack jumped up, furiously trying to flick the creature off him. As it landed on the floor, he stamped on the ground for good measure as a bat flew past and clipped the side of his ear.

***

A man was peering in every window of Ghyll Church, looking for Jack and his friends. "No. This door is locked, too," he heard one of his men call out. Where could they be, they had to be around here somewhere.

Looking towards the church grounds the man gawped in shock.

It was like watching a Satanic Mount Vesuvius, a black ashen, writhing, deafening hoard, spewed out of the ground. Against the backdrop of the fading skyline, a hoard of bats flew heavenwards.

"So it looks like you have been busy," the man smiled. It was only a matter of time. The treasure he had been craving for so long would soon be his.

And, getting rid of the evidence? That was what he did best! (13)

Chapter Twenty Nine

T

The three needed to press on. The damp was beginning to chill the inside of Jack's lungs with every breath. Each step seemed to take him further and further down into the belly of the tomb.

"Stop!" BT warned. "I know this is going to sound daft. But the walls look wrong, somehow."

"The only thing wrong is your head," Jack forced a laugh, trying to cheer up the situation.

"He's right," agreed Jules.

"What that BT's head is wrong?" Jack jumped in quickly.

"No, you idiot, BT is right! It shows a load of dots on the photo. I thought the picture was just grainy," replied Jules.

"Look at the floor. Some of the stone blocks are round," Jack observed.

"Whatever you do, don't stand on them," warned Jules.

"Why not?" asked Jack.

"Because, my wise friend, if you do, methinks the holes in the walls are booby trapped, and stepping on the wrong spot will trigger deadly arrows tipped with poison. The poison will probably kill you in ten seconds and if not, I will.

On the other hand, I could be completely wrong

and you're free to step on them. Either way I'll leave the choice up to you," Jules smirked.

"What if it's a double trick and the round bits are safe and the rest of the ground isn't?" Jack reasoned.

"We're not in some Indiana Jones film now, where the floor will collapse leaving a molten river flowing underneath. I'm guessing the round stones will be connected to some medieval mechanism. You stand on one of them and an arrow or thrusting spear will fire from those holes."

Jack decided to heed Jules' advice. He had nearly made it safely across the patchwork floor when Jules halted. BT collided with her stepping backwards only for Jack to bump into the back of BT.

It all happened so fast Jack was unable to react and tumbled backwards. A vision of the round stones entered his mind as he hit the ground. His elbow landed slap bang on one of the round stones.

BT apologised and was just about to bend down to help Jack up when Jules stopped him.

"Don't move," she shouted.

Three poisoned arrows flew out from the wall. Jack's heart almost stopped as they whistled inches from his face, before thudding into the opposite wall.

Jack froze. Every muscle locked. He was unable to move. After what seemed an eternity, a hand grabbed him and pulled him up.

"I've had it with all of this... that was too much," Jack moaned, getting back on his feet.

Then he saw why Jules had stopped. They had entered into another chamber. A new challenge faced them. There were three different entranceways to choose from, with only one leading to the treasure. Jack dared not think what dangers lay ahead for those who veered down the wrong path – at least they had a picture of the map.

"What was that?" Jack asked, positive he heard a noise.

"What was what? There's nothing there," Jules replied.

She was right – as always. His brain must be running in imagination top gear.

Then the same noise sounded again. There was someone here.

The shadows moved.

"Look out," shouted BT. "Ambush!"

All hell broke loose as a mass of bodies appeared out of nowhere. It was impossible to see who was who. Someone grabbed BT while Jack fell into the wall, smashing his torch.

Jack heard Jules scream. Before he could move towards her, a hand grabbed him.

He kicked out with all his might.

Free, he ran straight through the first available opening. Jack bolted into the passageway. He stumbled along blindly fighting his way through sticky cobwebs. On and on he ran with no end in sight, into pitch-blackness.

Anything was better than having the thugs catch him. Jack was confused, how had the bad guys overtaken them? Now he knew who stole the box, which carried the map, from his house!

In the darkness, he banged into a cold wall. Gritting his teeth, he winced from the pain in his arm.

It was then he realised, that it was a dead end. He fumbled around in the dark, kicking himself for making the wrong choice.

He was no longer in a passageway, but in some sort of chamber. Jack stopped to catch his breath. His heavy breathing competed with his heart for bragging rights for the loudest noise. A droplet of sweat rolled down the side of his cheek.

He stood enveloped in darkness. With any luck, no one had seen which way he had run.

Jack was sure he saw a light flicker in the distance before disappearing.

The light appeared again, only this time it did not vanish, it was heading his way. Someone was coming...

Jack had nowhere to go, nowhere to hide. He was trapped!

The light grew steadily brighter, lighting up what he now realised was a large, round chamber with a domed ceiling. Jack frantically searched around but could not see another way out.

Jack's gaze eventually rested on a table that

resembled the kitchen table from home. This one was made of stone rather than pine and sat in the middle of the underground tomb. On top of the table was a skeleton.

The spine-chilling dead bones resembled something from a scene in a horror movie. The figure lay stretched out solemnly, its bony fingers clasped around the ornate hilt of a sword.

Staring at it, he found it hard to resist, drawn to the skeleton like a snake to its charmer.

The design on the hilt of the sword was the cross of the four corners. Shimmering in the approaching light a golden crown encrusted with jewels sat crookedly on the skull.

Any second now and his assailant would be entering the chamber. He slouched down against the wall; curling himself up into a small ball in the vague hope, he would remain hidden.

The footsteps grew louder magnified by the underground amphitheatre.

"Jack, where are you? I know you are in here." Jack recognised the voice. Martin must have made it to safety and returned with the cavalry. He was saved!

Relieved, Jack jumped up, "I'm here."

The torch shone in his eyes, he tried to shield them with his hand.

"How did you find me?" he asked determined not to sound scared.

"Don't worry; everything is going to be alright."

"Did you come with the police? How did you manage to get past those guys?" Jack asked.

"All I need is for you to give me the key," said Simon.

"T-the key. Y-you? It c-can't be you! I thought it was Danny Pullen," Jack stuttered.

"Yes, Danny does seem the type. But he hasn't got the stomach for it," Simon sneered.

"But I heard him threatening you, at your house."

"What?" Simon laughed. "He wasn't threatening me, he wouldn't dare. He wanted you nosey kids out of the equation so he could carry out my business in peace. You were getting too close. You see, Danny works for me and that is my shop."

"You mean you've been after the Four Corners treasure all along?" Jack was curious, but also realised the longer he kept Holly's uncle talking, the more chance Martin would return with help.

"My, you have been little bees haven't you? As part of my line of work, I travel around the world looking for antiquities. A few years ago, I stumbled across an old legend regarding King Richard the Second and the Four Corners; he had taken some of their wealth and hidden it for his own purpose.

I don't know if you kids are brilliant or just damn lucky, but what's taken me years to figure out, you managed in a couple of weeks. But what I don't understand is, this stupid map is telling me to come down this tunnel, but it's a dead end."

"What, you stole the box?"

Simon stepped closer.

"I was probably right the first time – just damn lucky. It's such a pity we didn't meet under different circumstances; you seem such a bright boy. But as it is give-me-the-key."

If ever Jack needed a miracle, it was now. He got one...sort of. The battery in Simon's torch died. The odds had evened themselves out giving Jack a fighting chance.

Silently, Jack tried to take a step slowly back towards the wall, putting as much distance as possible between himself and Simon.

Jack inched around the edge of the room, carefully feeling his way against the outer wall with his fingertips. It was almost impossible to tell where Simon was, the underground room played tricks with the sounds. He prayed he would find the exit.

"I know you're there, young Jack Hunter," the voice echoed through the blackness.

Silently Jack spun around and set off in the opposite direction.

Jack inched further away only to inadvertently step on a dry root. It cracked louder than a gunshot with the sound bouncing off every wall in the echoing chamber.

Before Jack could move, he felt a pair of rough, strong hands grab his arms. He tried to escape, but

Simon's hands were too powerful.

"Did you really think you could escape from me?" Simon sniggered. "The gallant efforts of you and your little friends have been such a waste of my valuable time. Finally, I will get what's rightfully mine... while you...

I'm afraid, Jack Hunter... You lose!" (9)

Chapter Thirty

H

Jack wrestled free from Simon's grasp. Before he could make his escape, Simon pushed him. Jack fell against the stone table. Pain ripped through his shoulder and down his arm. There was no escape.

Jack wished he could be home with his mum and dad, safe and sound. If they had stayed in Southend, none of this would be happening.

Then Jack remembered the sword. His hand desperately clawed the pile of bones. Just the thought of touching a dead man's skeleton made him squeamish. The cold chamber reeked of death.

With that thought in mind, Jack's fingertips reached out. They touched something ice cold, not bone, but cold metal. The man's vicelike grip seized his right arm and Jack sensed he was too late.

Simon was trying to bind Jack's hands behind his back. Already he could feel the rope around his left wrist. Any second now, it would be all over. His grandad's life was at stake, he was desperate to succeed.

***

Simon was on the verge of fulfilling his dream. No kid was going to stop him!

He firmly held onto Jack pulling back the boys right arm. Within seconds, he would have the pest tied up, and with his accomplices sorting the other kids, he would have overcome the last thorn in his side.

For some reason Simon's body felt unusually warm. The damp, darkness that enveloped him in the tomb had chilled him to the bone; it was strange how warmth suddenly infused his body.

Ping!

Like a delayed email from a crashed server, a message suddenly arrived. It landed into his inbox. It simply read, 'You have a sharp pain, you are hurt!' End of message.

***

Jack felt his assailant's vice-like grip loosen. Seconds later, the man's grasp on Jack's arm relaxed. Jack's arms throbbed as the blood flow attempted to return to his wrists. The sound of his attacker staggering was the cue for Jack's escape. Blindly, he ran in the direction his mind pictured the exit. He was free!

A hand clawed at his ankle. It was enough to throw Jack off balance; gravity took over. He was helpless as he tumbled towards the stone table.

He had just rolled to a stop when he felt the floor give way underneath him.

He was falling.

Jack hit the ground with a thud. Everything around him turned cloudy. Jack was being whirled into a vortex of unconsciousness. The screaming in his head stopped. He could no longer fight the pain.

Everything went black. (6)

Chapter Thirty One

E

"Come in." Crackle. "Is there anybody there? Over."

Jack dreamed he stood underneath a buzzing wasps nest hanging on a branch.

"Come in. Over..."

Jack had no clue to his whereabouts. His body ached from head to toe. Everywhere was black.

Slowly he pushed his hands onto the damp floor where he lay and forced his exhausted body to move. The pain in his shoulder was almost unbearable.

The crackling noise was coming from the pocket of his jeans. It sounded like...of course, the walkie-talkie!

"Yeah...I-I'm re-ceiv-ing... Over," Jack stammered.

"Thank goodness you're there. Is that you, Jack? It's Holly... Over."

"Holly. I can't tell you how good it is to hear your voice," croaked Jack, trying to shake the cobwebs from his brain.

"Where are you, Jack? Over," said Holly

"I don't remember. Everywhere hurts."

"Copy that. Have you found the treasure? Over."

"No, I remember being in a room with your uncle..." Jack wished he could take that last word back.

"What do you mean, my uncle? Over."

"I don't know. I fell and banged my head and I can't really remember much. Are the others with you, Holly?"

"Negative. I haven't seen anyone since the bandits caught me. They tied me up. But they forgot to check my pockets. Good old Swiss army knife to the rescue. Over."

Jack wanted to believe the others were alright. A nagging voice in the back of his mind told him otherwise.

"I'm going to check out where I am. I'll come back to you in a minute. Oh and Holly, do me a favour and stop saying 'over'. You know it's me."

"Okay, good bud," replied Holly, "Roger that."

Lost and blind in the dark passageway, Jack had a thought. He rummaged through his pockets in hope. In the very last pocket his hand grabbed something small and round. He was in luck, the key ring torch!

At least Jack could see where he was going. He found himself standing at the beginning of a tunnel. It had a tall domed ceiling and walls made from wooden panelling with tapestries hanging and suits of armour. It seemed surreal considering how far underground he was.

He tried to remember how he had gotten there. His memory slowly trickled back, the scuffle with Simon and the dead kings' sword. Then as he made his escape, he tripped and bashed his head against the stone table. Finally he tumbled underneath the table and everything blacked out.

Jack looked up, directly overhead, there was a door in the roof. Hidden under the table must have been a trapdoor that had sprung open when he landed on it.

The chamber was not a dead end after all. He was on the right track.

The small beam from his key ring flickered. The battery was running low. With a deep breath, he placed one foot forward and set off along the passage. He could see only a few inches ahead, but kept going. Eventually he came to a dead end.

Just as he wondered if he had missed something he realised he was facing a door.

There was no way to open it. It had no handle or keyhole. He stared at it in the light. It had the cross of the four corners carved into its centre. An image flashed in his mind of Jules pressing the diamond on the gravestone. Jack pressed down hard on the shape in the centre of the cross.

The symbol flipped open to reveal a lock. After searching through every pocket again, he finally withdrew the old, bronze key. Now he understood why Simon was so desperate to get his hands on the key.

His hand was trembling. Slowly Jack inserted the key into the lock, turned it left, and then right. Just as before, a small hatch flipped open.

Inside the compartment was a metal triangle – like the ones you get in music class – only this had one corner made from gold. He pulled out the prize. It was a bit feeble after all the effort he and his friends had put in. He slammed the compartment shut.

To Jack's surprise the door swung open.

Jack stepped through the doorway but instead of a room full of treasure, there was just more of the same boring tunnel.

A crackle buzzed from his pocket. "Jack! Jack! Come in. Over. Er, sorry. I mean, well, are you blinking well there or what?" It was Holly.

"Yeah, mate, what's up?" Jack heard his voice bouncing back down from the vaulted ceiling.

"Good news," Holly announced. "The police are here, and guess what? Your grandad is here as well. He's safe and sound. Over. Whoops, sorry..."

"What? He is? Can I speak to him?" shouted Jack.

"I'm here sonny Jim. Hello, Jack... are you there? I can't hear you. This flaming contraption doesn't work!" Grandad turned to Holly.

For a minute, Jack was lost for words. "Er, yeah, grandad, I'm here. I thought those thugs had..." stammered Jack.

"Him? He was no match for my trusty walking stick and me. Never even thought to take it off me. What a Neanderthal!" chuckled his grandad.

"I think I'm in that same tunnel you found, grandad. I think I can see the cave-in up ahead," reported Jack.

"You see? I knew you'd do it!" exclaimed the old man, "Listen we're comin'..."

The line abruptly went dead. Jack shouted repeatedly. The battery had died.

Jack squeezed past the mound of rubble that had filled in most of the tunnel. A flashback from his grandad's story caused his heart to beat even faster. Then he saw it, only a few yards away, just as his grandad had described.

The lid of the timeless wooden casket fell back as Jack opened it. Even in the near black tunnel, this was the most amazing sight he had ever seen. Every colour imaginable glistened brightly every time he waved the small torch. Diamonds, emerald broaches, ruby tiaras and pearl necklaces entwined amongst a mountain of gold coins. Jack picked out a gold coin just as his grandad had done many years before.

The coin slipped from his clammy hand. He heard it bounce on the stone floor before rolling away. He was desperate not to lose the coin; it was too valuable. Jack tracked the sound to where the coin had stopped. As he picked it up, he saw something unbelievable. Jack froze in sheer wonder. The wooden box was not the only treasure in the tunnel.

Before he had chance to absorb the new information, Jack heard a strange rumbling sound – a sort of grumble-in-your-belly-when-you're-hungry-kind-of-noise, except a lot louder. The whole tunnel began to vibrate. A terrible thought crossed his mind. What if Simon and his cronies had found him?

The whole world around him was shuddering violently. The ceiling exploded just feet from him. Light flooded into the tunnel from above. Rubble tumbled from the sky. A clod of soil smacked Jack squarely on the chin, sending him sprawling to the ground.

He could hear voices. His eyes struggled to focus. He could see shapes dropping through the hole. Everything was a blur. The walls were beginning to spin. Jack tried to fight against the vertigo. This was so unfair; the bad guys could not be allowed to win. He had to defend the treasure—no matter what.

All went black...again! (18)

Chapter Thirty Two

L

A bright light briefly blinded Jack as he opened his eyes. Shapes around him took on features as his vision slowly returned. Then he recognised his grandad's crinkly face smiling down at him.

"Where is he?" a familiar voice called from behind his grandad. "Where's Indiana Jones the Second?" shouted Holly.

Jack bolted upright. Although he felt dizzy, a happy feeling washed over him. "Be careful, Jack. Don't you go moving about," his concerned grandad cautioned.

"Careful please. Don't crowd him, we need to get him to the hospital," shouted an unknown voice. Jack smiled; adults would never learn that kids were indestructible.

It turned out grandad had beaten the baddie with his walking stick before raising the alarm.

"Holly, you alright?" Holly smiled.

"What about the others?" Jack suddenly remembered, "Martin, Jules and BT? Where are they? They were being chased," he muttered.

Before he could open his mouth, the three of them came charging into view. Jack sat up properly in time to receive a high five from Martin. Jules gave him a quick kiss on his cheek.

"Yuk! Girls!" Jack said rubbing his cheek. Everyone laughed.

A thought occurred to him. "But how did you know where I was? I mean, how did you find me?" he asked.

"Please move back. He's in no condition for all these questions," called one of the paramedics. The man gently pushed Jack back down.

"That was the easy part," BT grinned, squeezing past all the bodies surrounding Jack. "I used my dad's homemade Bakertech ultrasonic tracking system with a little tweaking by yours truly for insular movement. I installed one in each watch, in case we got trapped or lost so my dad could find us."

BT made no sense to Jack; all he knew was that BT was a genius. In fact, they all were in their own way. Together they made the perfect team. Nothing could beat them.

Jack strained his head to peer over the adults to suddenly realise they were in the middle of what he could only describe as a war zone. From the temporary floodlights, he could see people milling about everywhere. Firemen, police—in fact, probably half of Barnoldswick were there. There was a small JCB digger, fire trucks, police cars and an ambulance. And all of this in the middle of a golf course!

"We've found the treasure." Jack heard someone call out.

"Looks like you're in for a big reward," Inspector

Tyrrell, who seemed to appear out of nowhere, said to Jack. As Jack's eyes tried to take in everything that was happening, he saw an odd-looking man standing in the background, away from the chaos. The hood from the cloak he wore hid the man's features.

"Wow, look at all this gold," a young policeman said, briefly distracting Jack's gaze and when he looked back, the hooded man had vanished.

"There must be millions of pounds of the stuff down here." Although Jack felt gutted that the police were taking away his treasure, at least the bad guys didn't get it. To Jack's surprise, he saw another policeman climb out of the hole with a treasure chest and then another and another.

Before the news could sink in, Jack saw Simon King stuffed into the rear of a police car. A wave of relief swept over him. He was thankful for not mortally wounding the man – although he definitely deserved it.

His mum and dad appeared from the crowd. "Oh luvvie, you're safe and sound," his mum cooed, before giving him a hug in front of everyone.

"Mum...I'm fine." How embarrassing!

"Oh good," she replied. "In that case, with the reward you're getting, you can buy me a new crystal ornament to replace the one you broke." (13)

Chapter Thirty Three

ID

Jack awoke to a strange smell – a sort of everywhere scrubbed clean with chemicals and mashed potatoes kind of smell. The room was bright and the metal framed bed creaked loudly as he moved. He almost thought he was still dreaming before realising where he was.

"So there's the war veteran..."

It was a voice he instantly recognised and sat up excitedly. His grandad walked towards him, his shoes squeaking louder than a dozen mice as he walked across the hospital floor. He held out what looked to be a bottle wrapped in a brown paper bag.

"Sarsaparilla," he said with a huge grin.

"Er, thanks grandad," Jack said not wanting to disappoint.

Within seconds, the two of them were reliving yesterday's amazing events. Jack still had a lot of unanswered questions and knew he needed to ask them quickly, before the nurse returned.

"But what I don't get grandad...is why Holly's uncle? I mean he seemed such a nice man. Even Holly said he could never have done anything like that. And I saw some bloke afterwards dressed all weird. It still feels like the secret is only half open."

"I think that bump on your head is playing tricks

with you son," his grandad chuckled.

"But I'm serious grandad. It doesn't make any sense."

"But the thing you've got to remember son is, not everything is as it appears."

"I don't understand what you mean?" Jack asked.

"What I mean is..."

"Jack!"

He looked up to see Holly, Martin, BT and Jules charging towards him.

"Are you going to hurry up and get out of here?" asked Martin.

"Martin, now don't be rude," his mum said.

"But the papers are waiting for him mum," he said before turning to Jack. "It's all anyone is talking about."

"That's right," said BT. "We're celebrities."

"The doctor reckons you'll be out tomorrow," said Jules.

"Come along now, out of my way! I've got a job to do," said the nurse.

***

Jack was up bright and early. Today was the first day at his new school. A whole week had passed since that incredible night. After his release from hospital – because in Jack's own words, 'there was nothing wrong with him,' – so much had happened.

For those few days, he felt like a celebrity.

He never normally got up this early for school, but today was an exception. He heard a knock at the door and was halfway down the stairs when it burst open and four excited children barged into the house.

"Well have you got it?" Jack asked.

"Of course," BT grinned waving the newspaper. Jules thrust a copy into Jack's hands.

"And it's not just the West Craven Chronicle," Martin pointed out. "It's in all the papers."

"Which page?" Jack asked frantically leafing through. "I can't find it."

"The front page," beamed Holly.

"It's on the front page?" Jack gasped.

"And page four," added Jules.

"And five," said BT.

"And..."

"Okay, I get it. Let me have a look," Jack cut Martin short. "Wow. It says here, 'After cracking numerous clues, on Saturday evening, Jack Hunter (12)' it says me first,"

"Shurrup and read it," said Martin.

"'And friends Martin Brown (12), Julie Brown (11), Shaun Hollingsworth (12) and Anthony Baker (10) of Barnoldswick, Lancashire, discovered the largest haul of medieval treasure in the UK, believed to be worth tens of millions of pounds.' Wow, is it really worth that much. Tens of millions, did you know?"

"Of course, I've read the article about fifteen times," bragged Holly.

"You need to read the bit about the reward the paper says we're gonna get too," Martin whooped. "What are you gonna spend it on? And how much do you think we're getting?"

"Have you read the bit where they interview me about my historical knowledge? They say I'm a child prodigy," boasted Holly.

As a one-off special treat – at least they were the exact words his mum had used – she had driven all the way to Colne and bought them a McDonald's breakfast. Jack did not care if it was cold by the time she returned. This was Jack's best ever morning.

The key and the letter found inside the brick from the barn had been given to the authorities. To prevent its deterioration, King Richard's note had been placed in a special airtight glass case. It was going to be part of an exhibit at the British Museum along with most of the haul.

Jack had kept the coin. He decided, as it was a present from his grandad, it was not actually stealing. He also kept the metal triangle; he had shown proudly for the newspaper photo shoot, because the authorities did not deem it valuable.

The triangle with the golden corner had two symbols near the bottom edge. The first was a circle with a twisted cross inside, almost as if someone who had been drunk had engraved it. The second looked like a little golf flag.

That was it. He was not sure, if it connected to the treasure they had discovered or a clue to something else, but he kept it safely hidden in his bedroom.

"School's going to be so much fun, don't you think?" said Holly as they strolled casually towards West Craven High Technology College. Why did everywhere in Barnoldswick have to have such long-winded names?

"School fool," Martin said mimicking Holly.

"Hey man, are you Jack Hunter?" shouted a tall red haired kid. The boy and his mates must have been at least fourteen or fifteen.

"Er, ye-ress... I am," stuttered Jack, unsure what they may to do to him.

"Cool, I knew it was, I saw your picture in the paper," he shouted before turning back to his friends he was with. "See I told you it was him."

Wow, Jack could not believe it. Things like this never happened to him. Southend was all but a distant memory and for the first time he could ever recall, life felt brilliant.

He was Jack Hunter!

The adventure continues...

Did you find the secret message hidden within these pages? To finish the puzzle and solve the mystery go to: www.martinkingauthor.com

Jack and his friends will return soon.

Lightning Source UK Ltd.
Milton Keynes UK
UKOW051432290312

189824UK00001B/4/P